MORE PRAISE FOR B

"Sassy, smart . . .
Babymouse is here
to stay."
—**The Horn Book Magazine**

"Young readers
will happily
fall in line."
—**Kirkus Reviews**

"The brother-sister creative team hits the mark
with humor, sweetness, and characters so genuine
they can pass for real kids." —**Booklist**

"Babymouse is spunky, ambitious,
and, at times, a total dweeb."
—**School Library Journal**

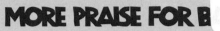

Be sure to read **all** the **BABYMOUSE** books:

#1 BABYMOUSE: Queen of the World!
#2 BABYMOUSE: Our Hero
#3 BABYMOUSE: Beach Babe
#4 BABYMOUSE: Rock Star
#5 BABYMOUSE: Heartbreaker
#6 CAMP BABYMOUSE
#7 BABYMOUSE: Skater Girl
#8 BABYMOUSE: Puppy Love
#9 BABYMOUSE: Monster Mash
#10 BABYMOUSE: The Musical
#11 BABYMOUSE: Dragonslayer
#12 BABYMOUSE: Burns Rubber
#13 BABYMOUSE: Cupcake Tycoon
#14 BABYMOUSE: Mad Scientist

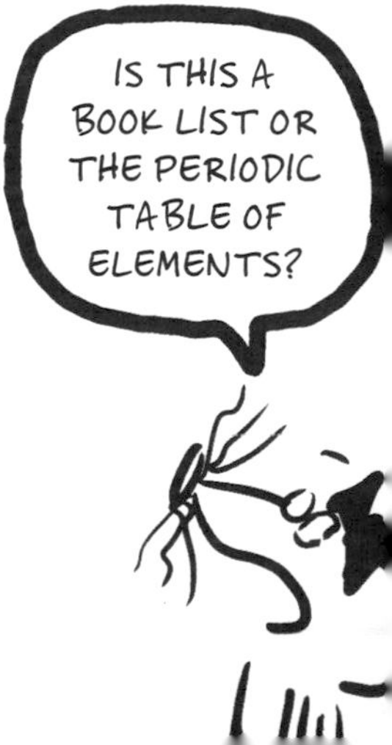
IS THIS A BOOK LIST OR THE PERIODIC TABLE OF ELEMENTS?

BABYMOUSE

MAD SCIENTIST

BY JENNIFER L. HOLM & MATTHEW HOLM

RANDOM HOUSE 🏠 NEW YORK

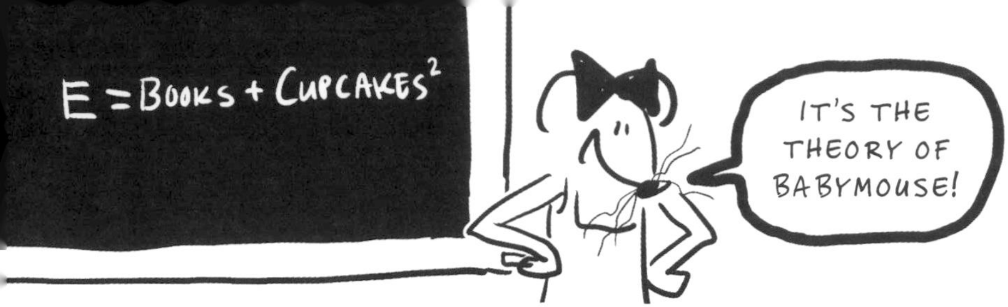
E = Books + Cupcakes²
IT'S THE THEORY OF BABYMOUSE!

This is a work of fiction. Names, characters, places, and incidents either are the product of the authors' imagination or are used fictitiously. Any resemblance to actual persons, living or dead, events, or locales is entirely coincidental.

Published in the United States by Random House Children's Books, a division of Random House, Inc., New York.

RANDOM HOUSE and the colophon are registered trademarks of Random House, Inc.

Visit us on the Web! www.randomhouse.com/kids
Babymouse.com

Educators and librarians, for a variety of teaching tools, visit us at www.randomhouse.com/teachers

Library of Congress Cataloging-in-Publication Data
Holm, Jennifer L.
Babymouse: mad scientist / by Jennifer L. Holm and Matthew Holm. — 1st ed.
p. cm.
Summary: Babymouse discovers Squish, a new species of amoeba, while working on a school science fair project.
ISBN 978-0-375-86574-9 (trade) — ISBN 978-0-375-96574-6 (lib. bdg.)
1. Graphic novels. [1. Graphic novels. 2. Amoeba—Fiction. 3. Science projects—Fiction. 4. Schools—Fiction. 5. Mice—Fiction.] I. Holm, Matthew. II. Title. III. Title: Mad scientist.
PZ7.7.H65Bag 2009 741.5'973—dc22 2009047388

MANUFACTURED IN MALAYSIA 10 9 8 7 6 5 4 3 2 1 First Edition

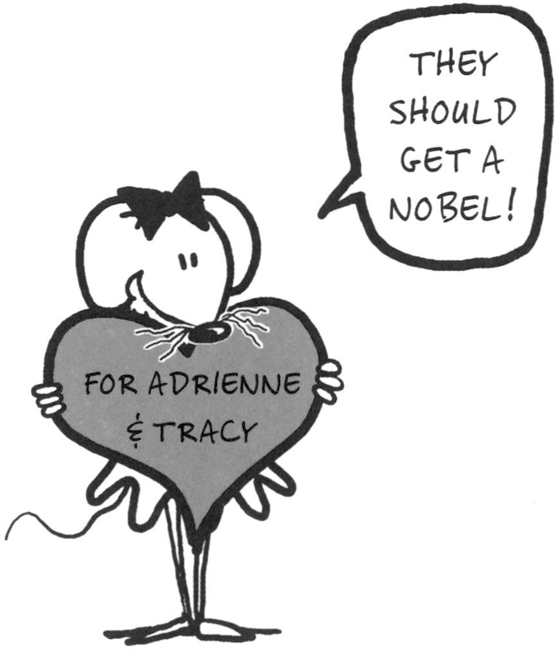
THEY SHOULD GET A NOBEL!
FOR ADRIENNE & TRACY

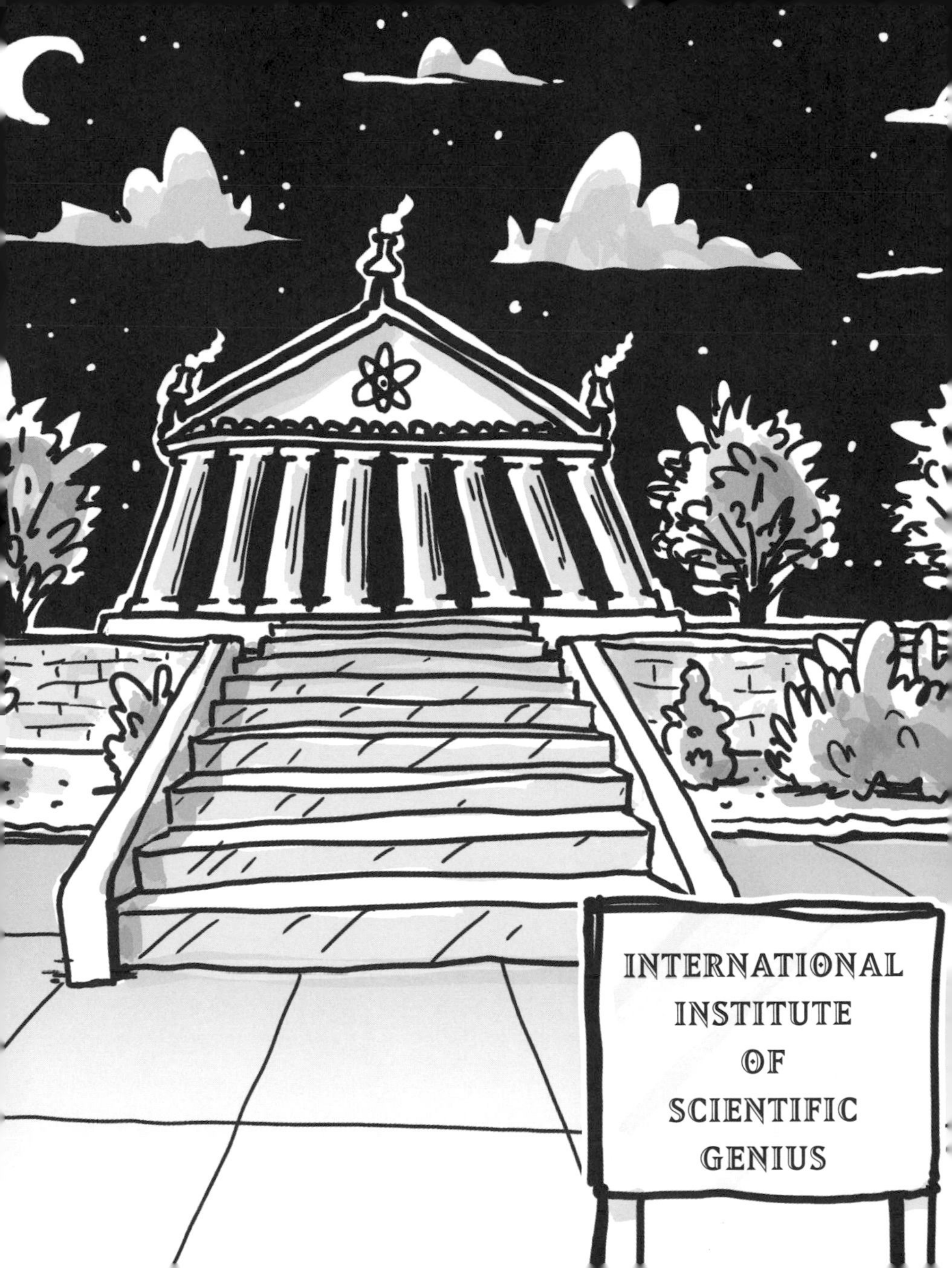
INTERNATIONAL
INSTITUTE
OF
SCIENTIFIC
GENIUS

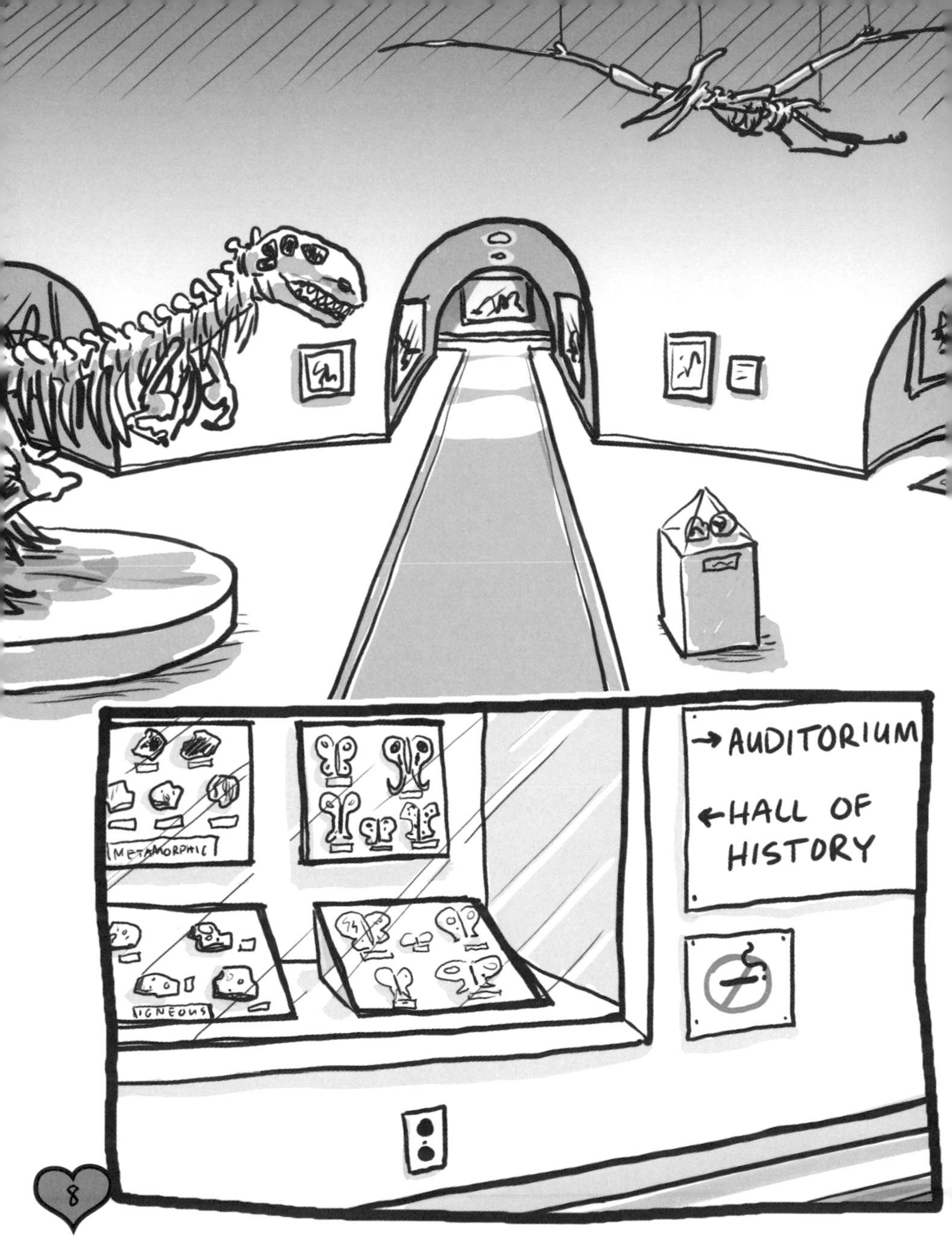
→AUDITORIUM
←HALL OF HISTORY
METAMORPHIC
IGNEOUS

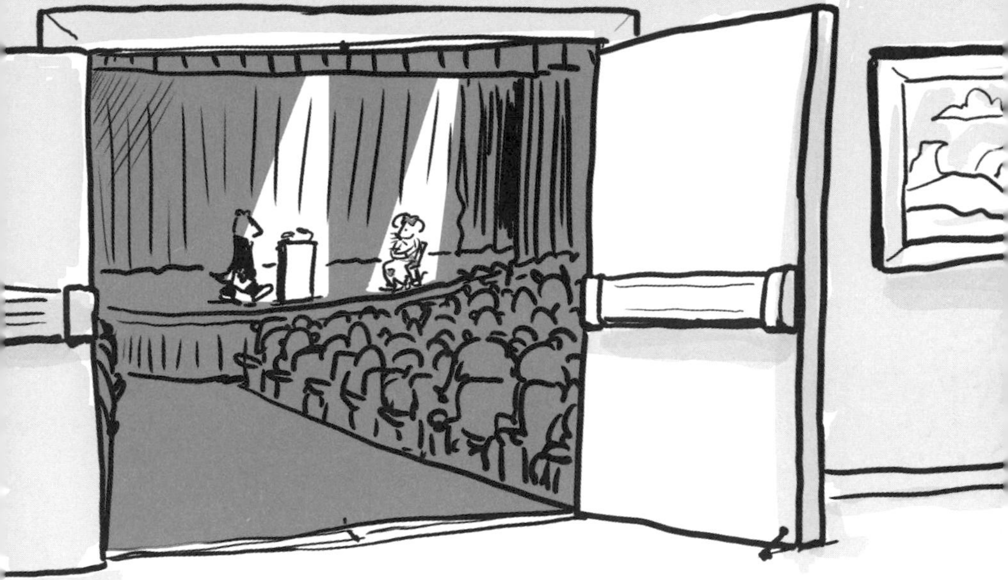

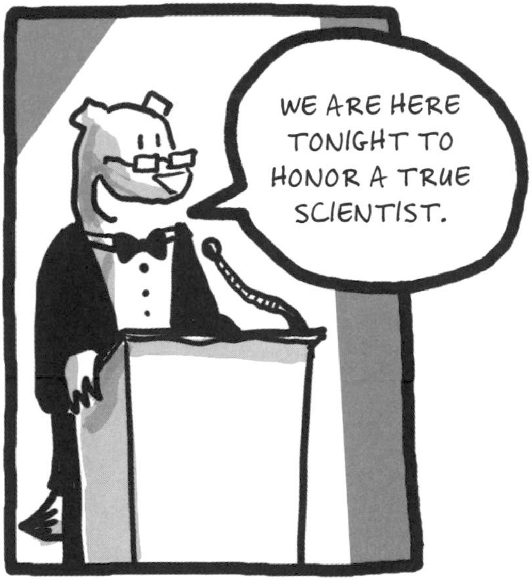
WE ARE HERE TONIGHT TO HONOR A TRUE SCIENTIST.

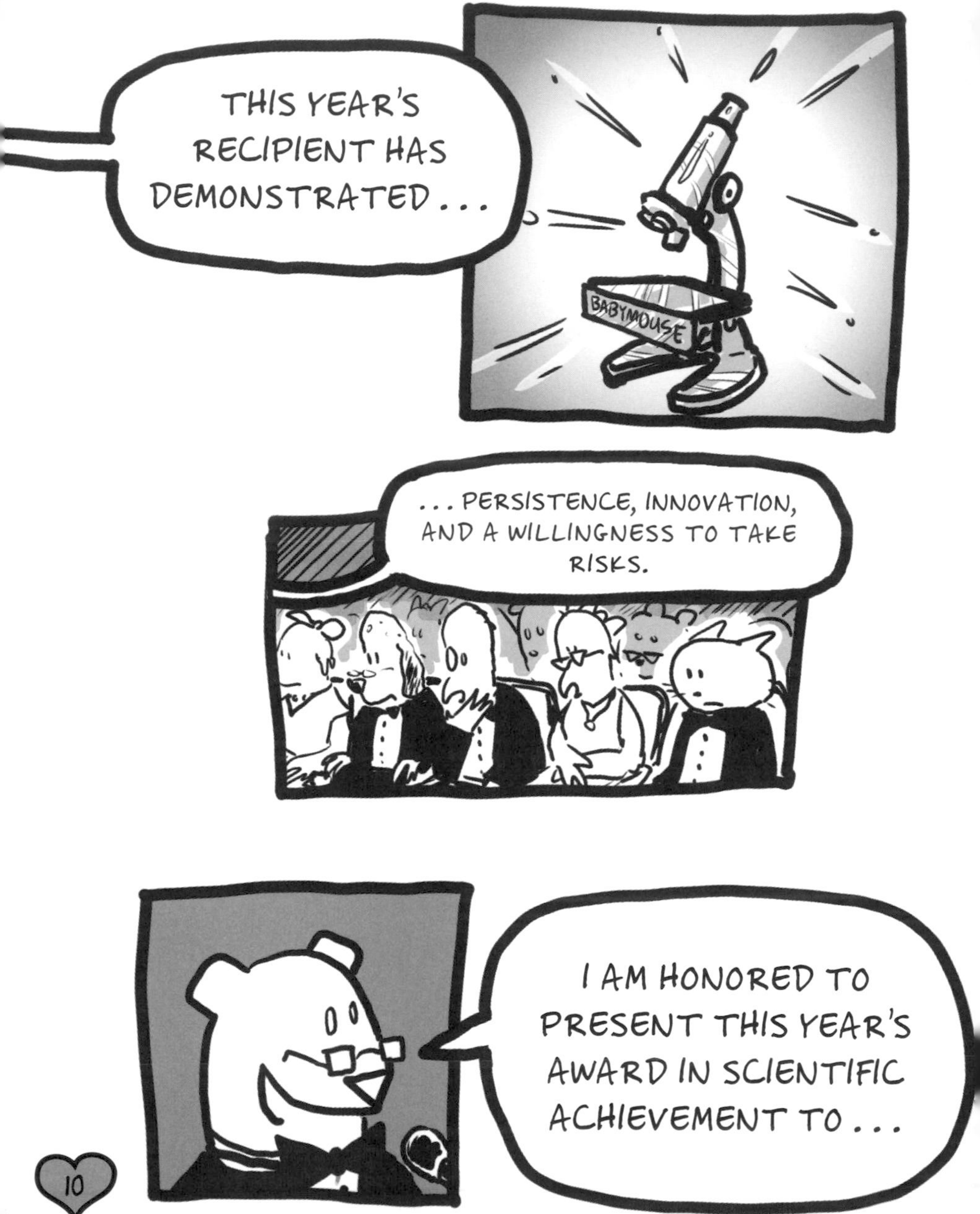
THIS YEAR'S RECIPIENT HAS DEMONSTRATED...
BABYMOUSE
...PERSISTENCE, INNOVATION, AND A WILLINGNESS TO TAKE RISKS.
I AM HONORED TO PRESENT THIS YEAR'S AWARD IN SCIENTIFIC ACHIEVEMENT TO...

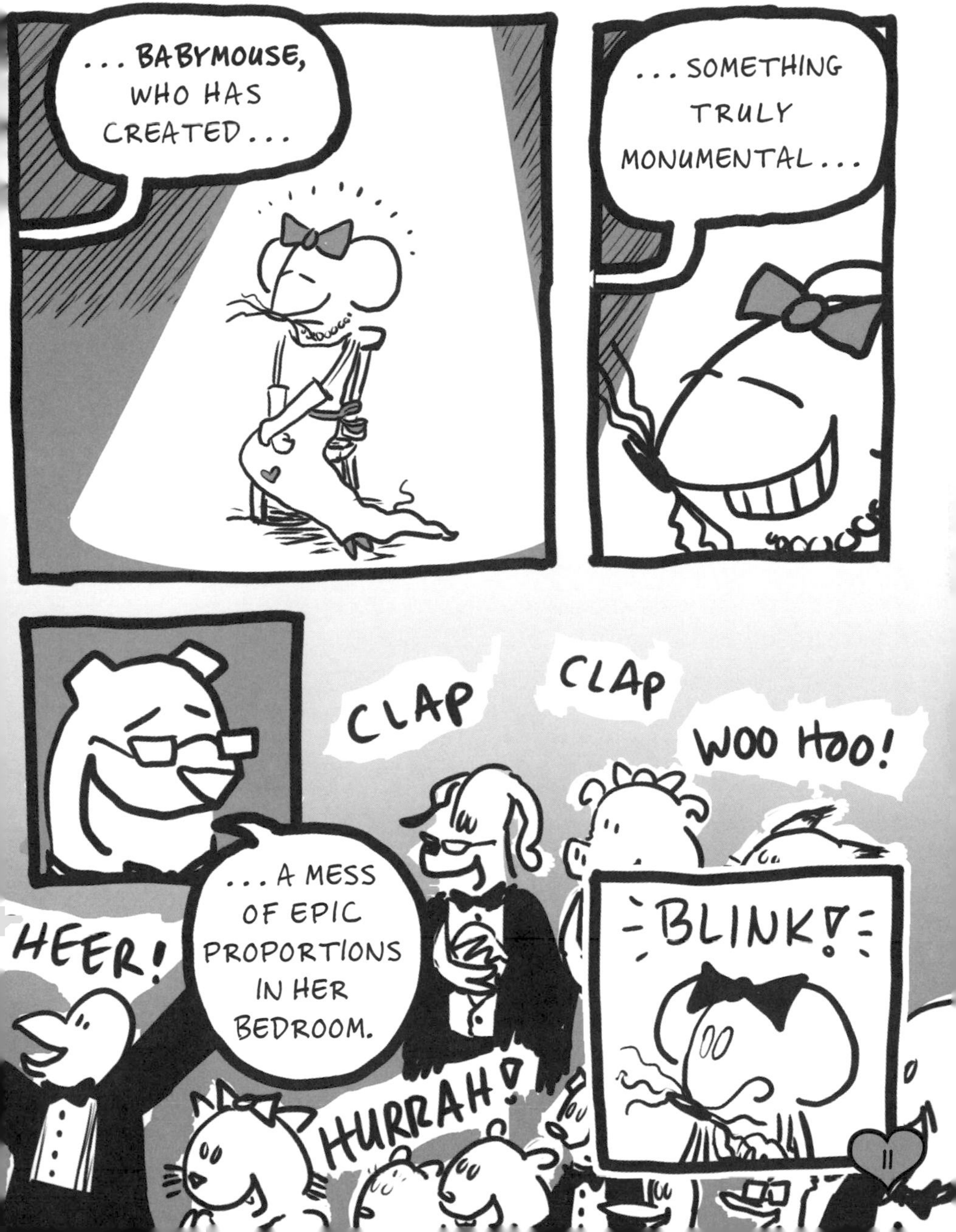
. . . BABYMOUSE, WHO HAS CREATED . . .
. . . SOMETHING TRULY MONUMENTAL . . .
CLAP
CLAP
WOO HOO!
. . . A MESS OF EPIC PROPORTIONS IN HER BEDROOM.
HEER!
BLINK!
HURRAH!

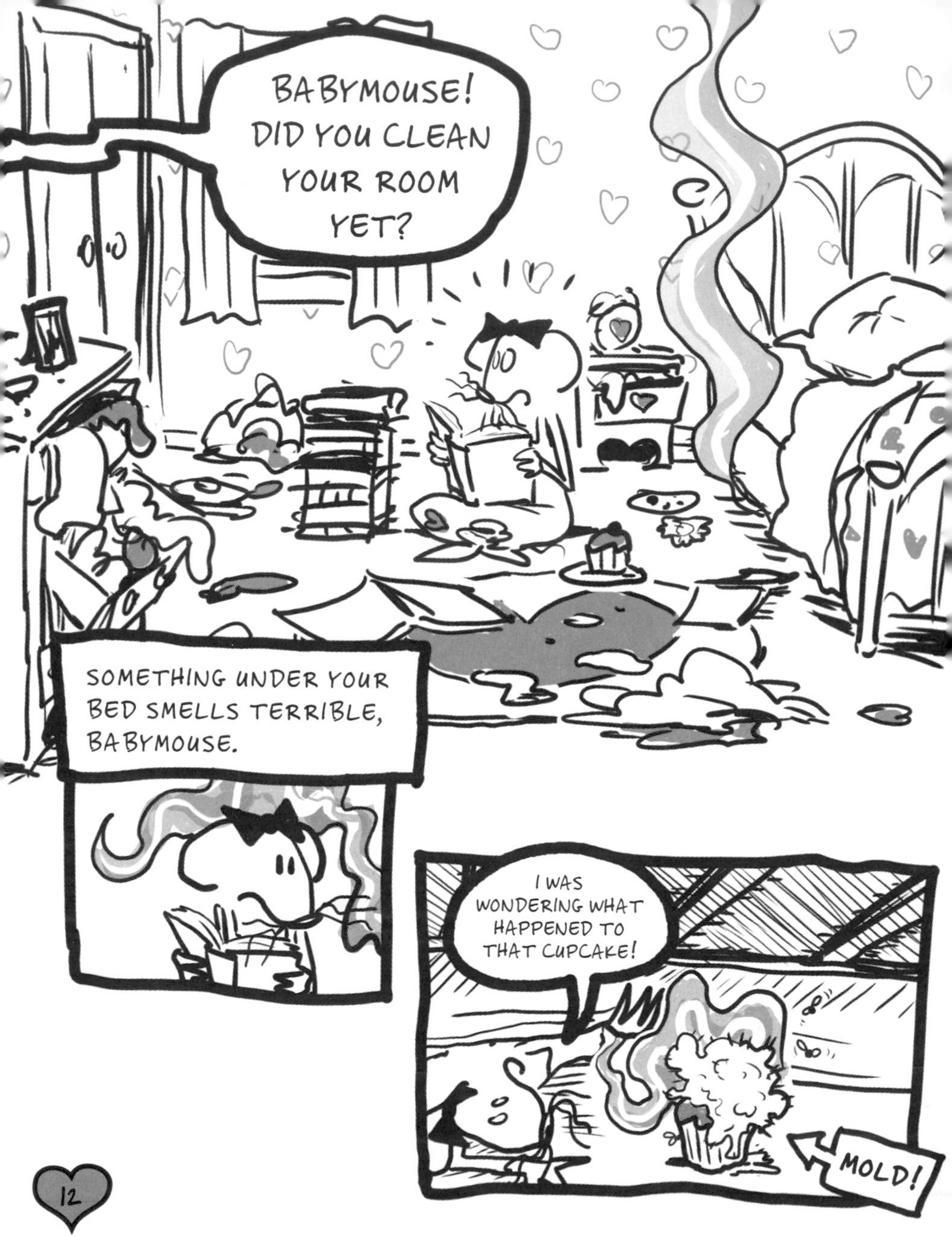

BABYMOUSE! DID YOU CLEAN YOUR ROOM YET?
SOMETHING UNDER YOUR BED SMELLS TERRIBLE, BABYMOUSE.
I WAS WONDERING WHAT HAPPENED TO THAT CUPCAKE!
MOLD!

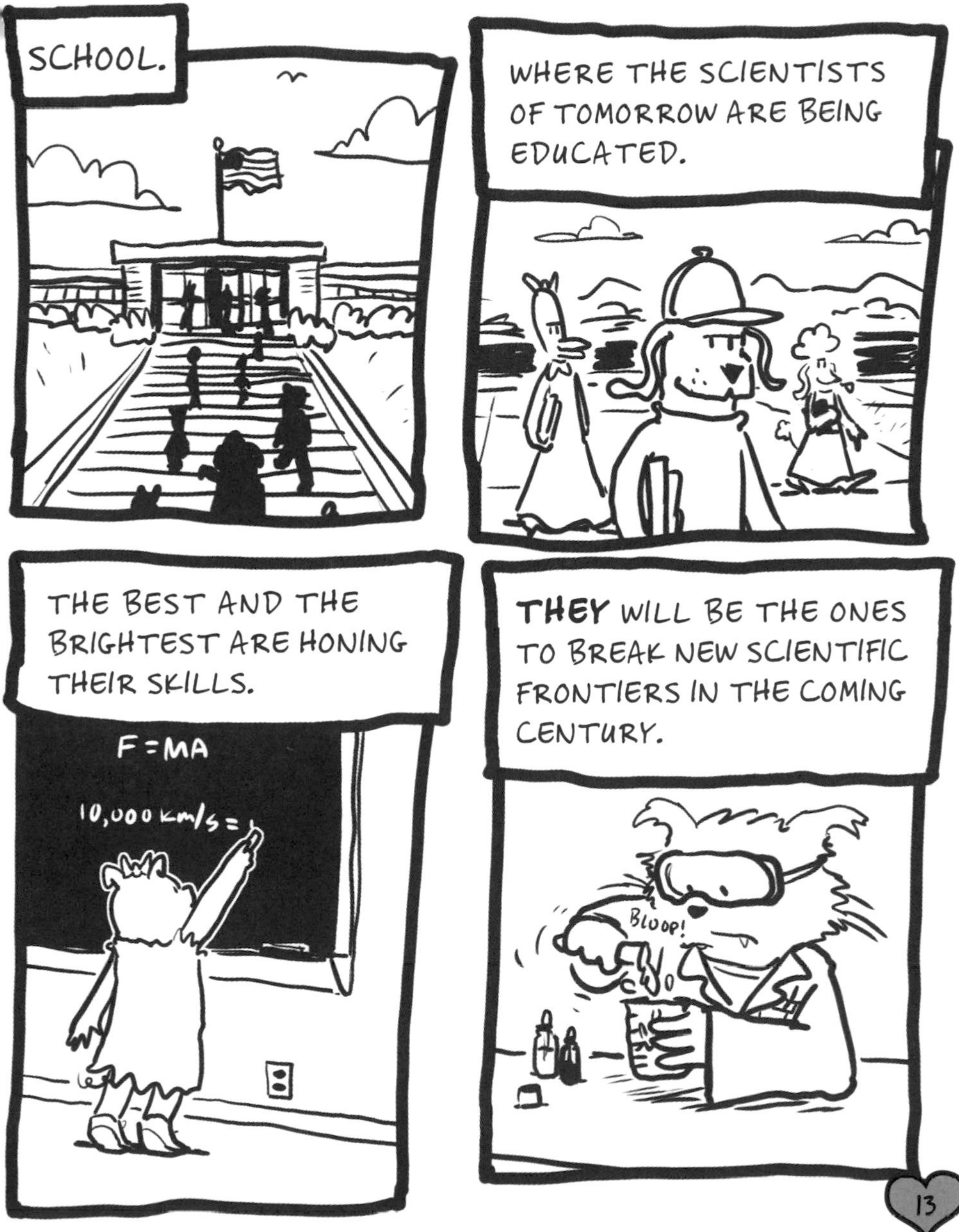
SCHOOL.
WHERE THE SCIENTISTS OF TOMORROW ARE BEING EDUCATED.
THE BEST AND THE BRIGHTEST ARE HONING THEIR SKILLS.
F=MA
10,000 km/s =
THEY WILL BE THE ONES TO BREAK NEW SCIENTIFIC FRONTIERS IN THE COMING CENTURY.
BLOOP!

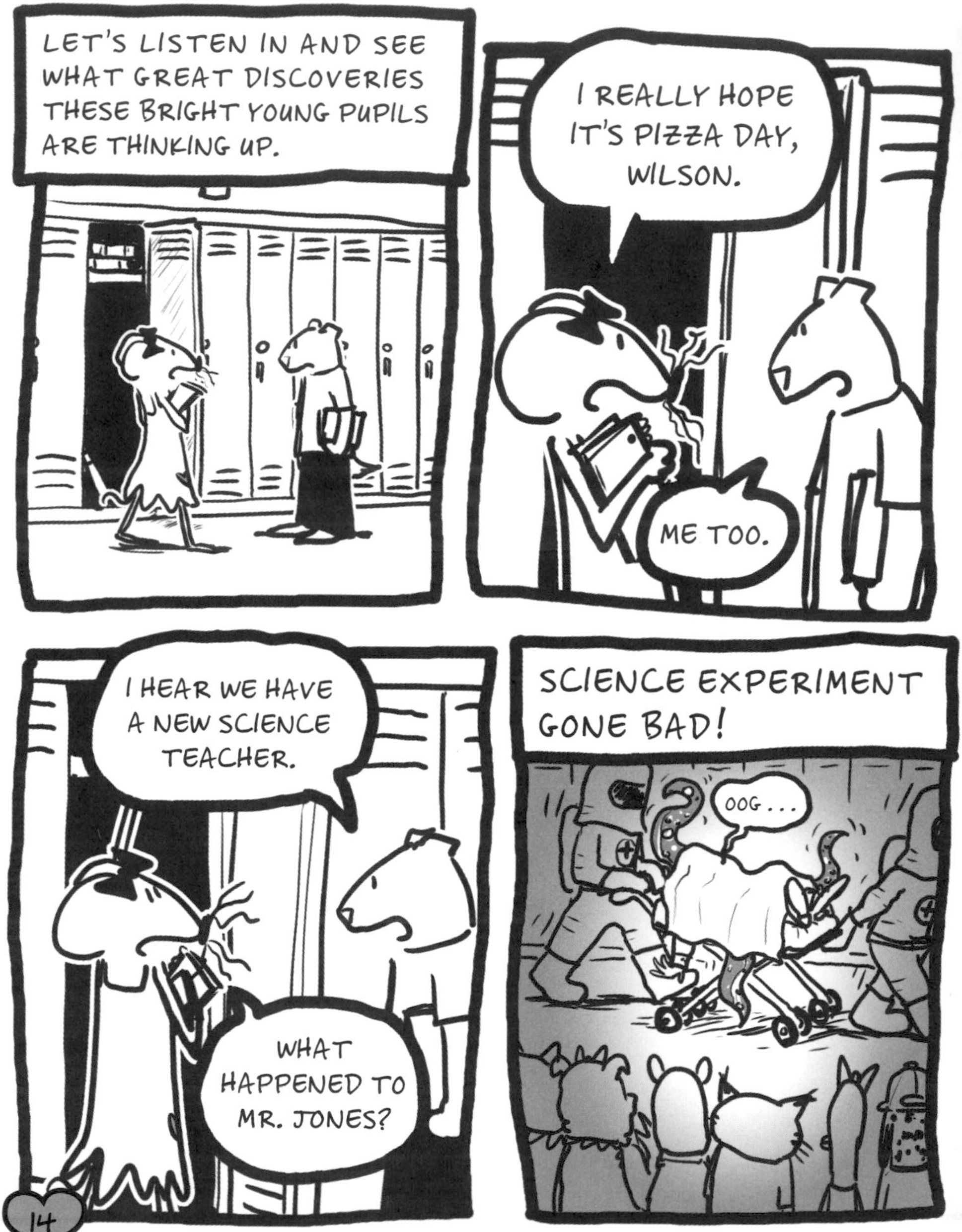
LET'S LISTEN IN AND SEE WHAT GREAT DISCOVERIES THESE BRIGHT YOUNG PUPILS ARE THINKING UP.
I REALLY HOPE IT'S PIZZA DAY, WILSON.
ME TOO.
I HEAR WE HAVE A NEW SCIENCE TEACHER.
WHAT HAPPENED TO MR. JONES?
SCIENCE EXPERIMENT GONE BAD!
OOG . . .

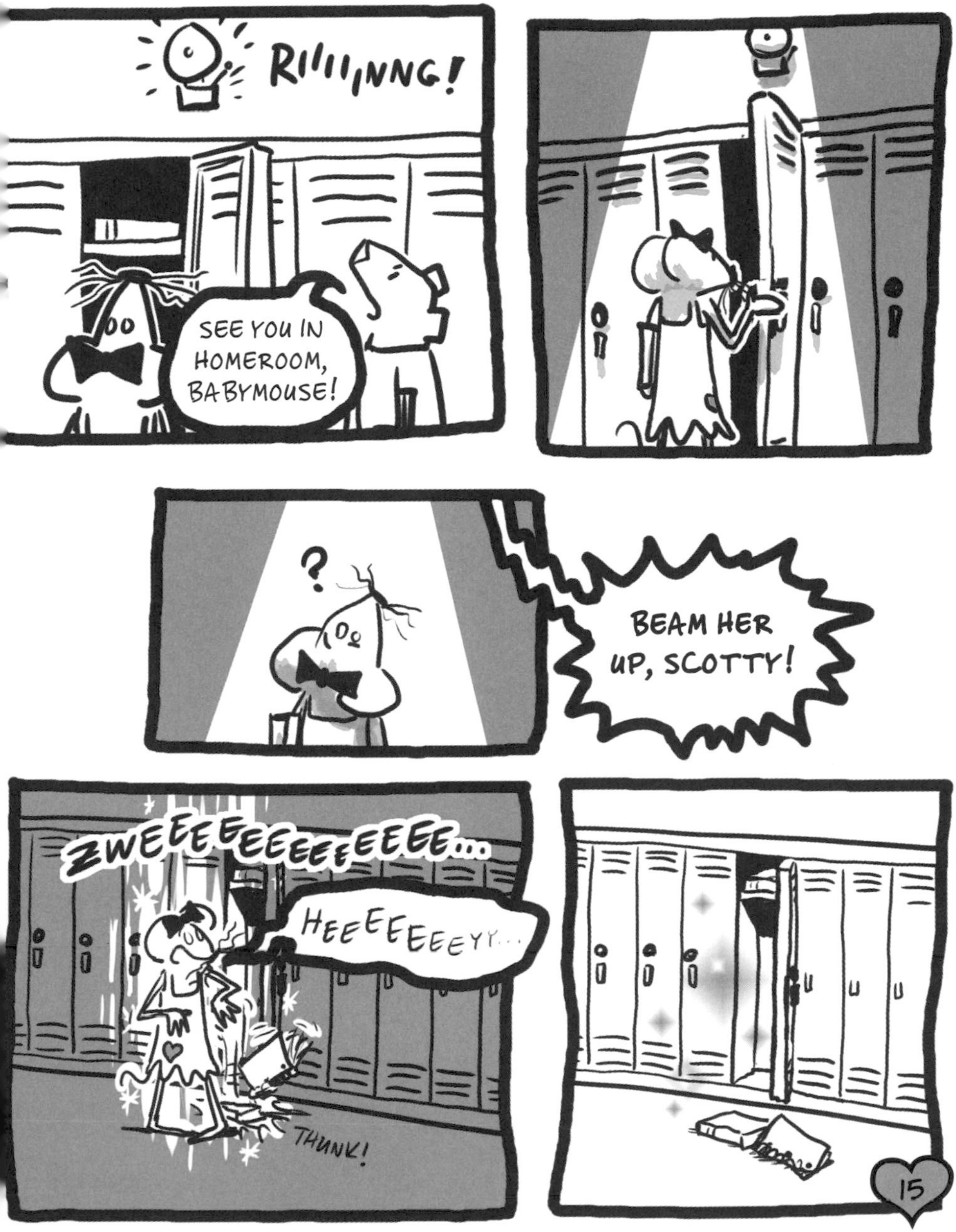

RIIIIINNG!
SEE YOU IN HOMEROOM, BABYMOUSE!
?
BEAM HER UP, SCOTTY!
ZWEEEEEEEEEEEEEE...
HEEEEEEEEYY...
THUNK!

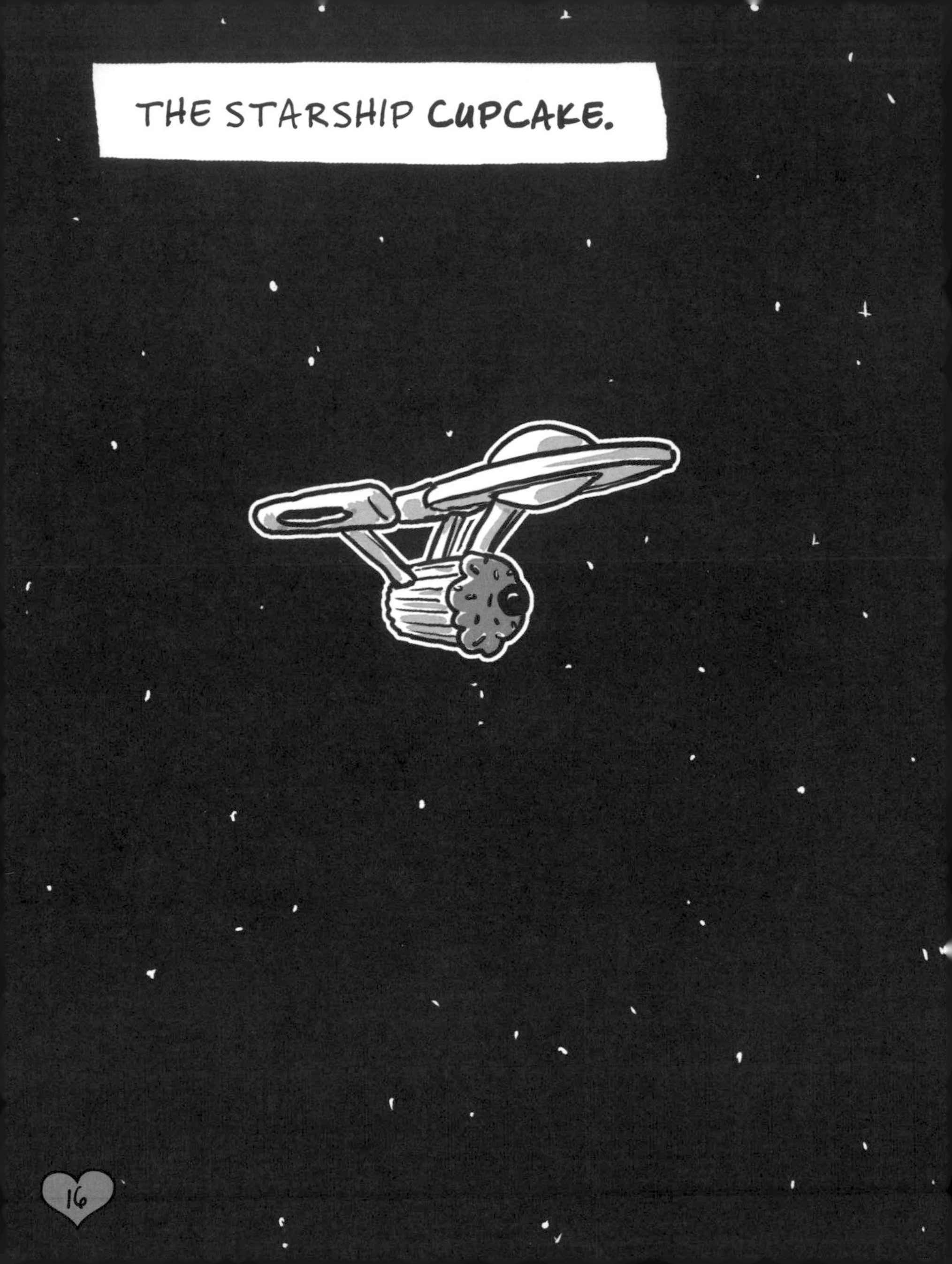
THE STARSHIP CUPCAKE.

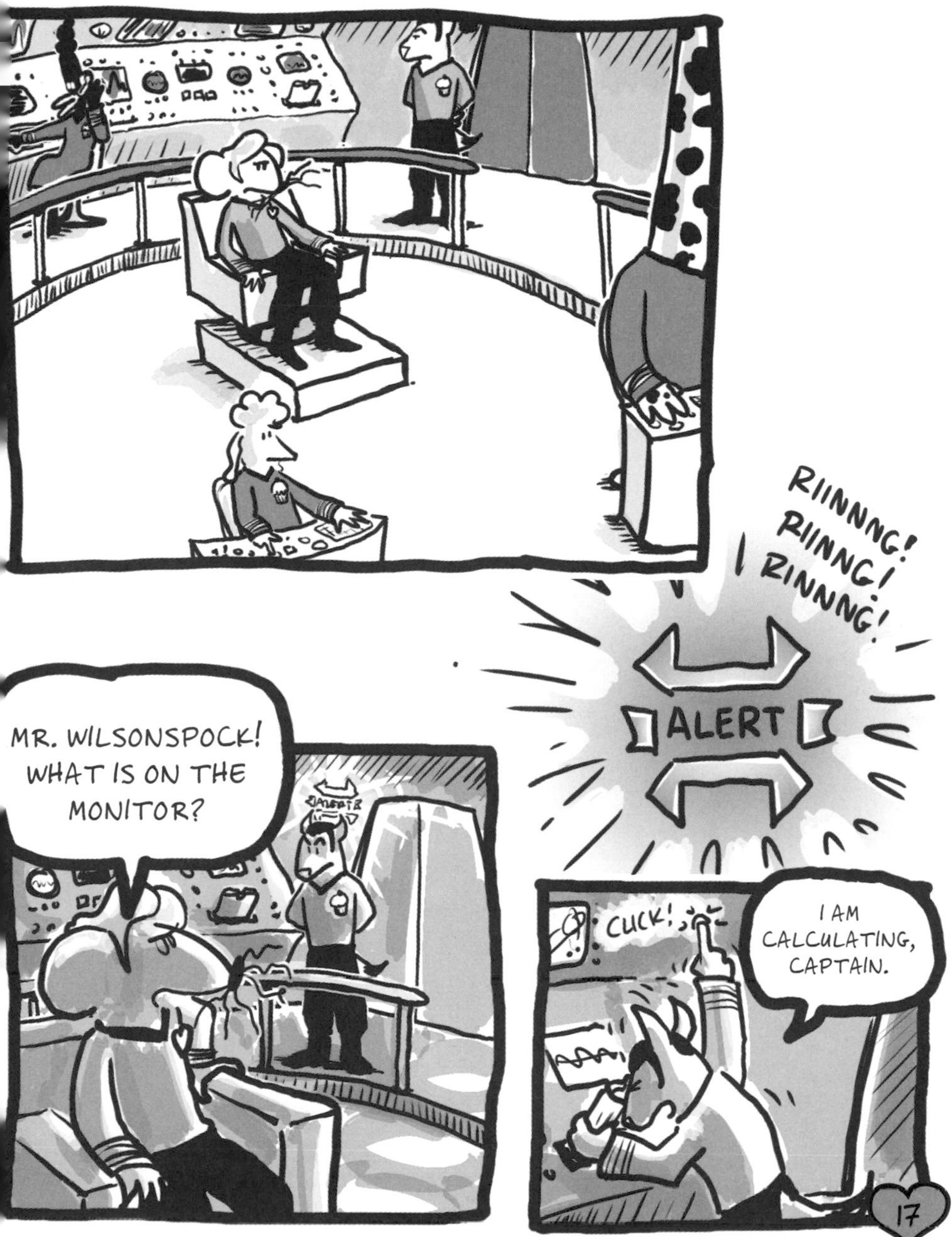
RIINNNG!
RIINNG!
RINNNG!
ALERT
MR. WILSONSPOCK! WHAT IS ON THE MONITOR?
CLICK!
I AM CALCULATING, CAPTAIN.

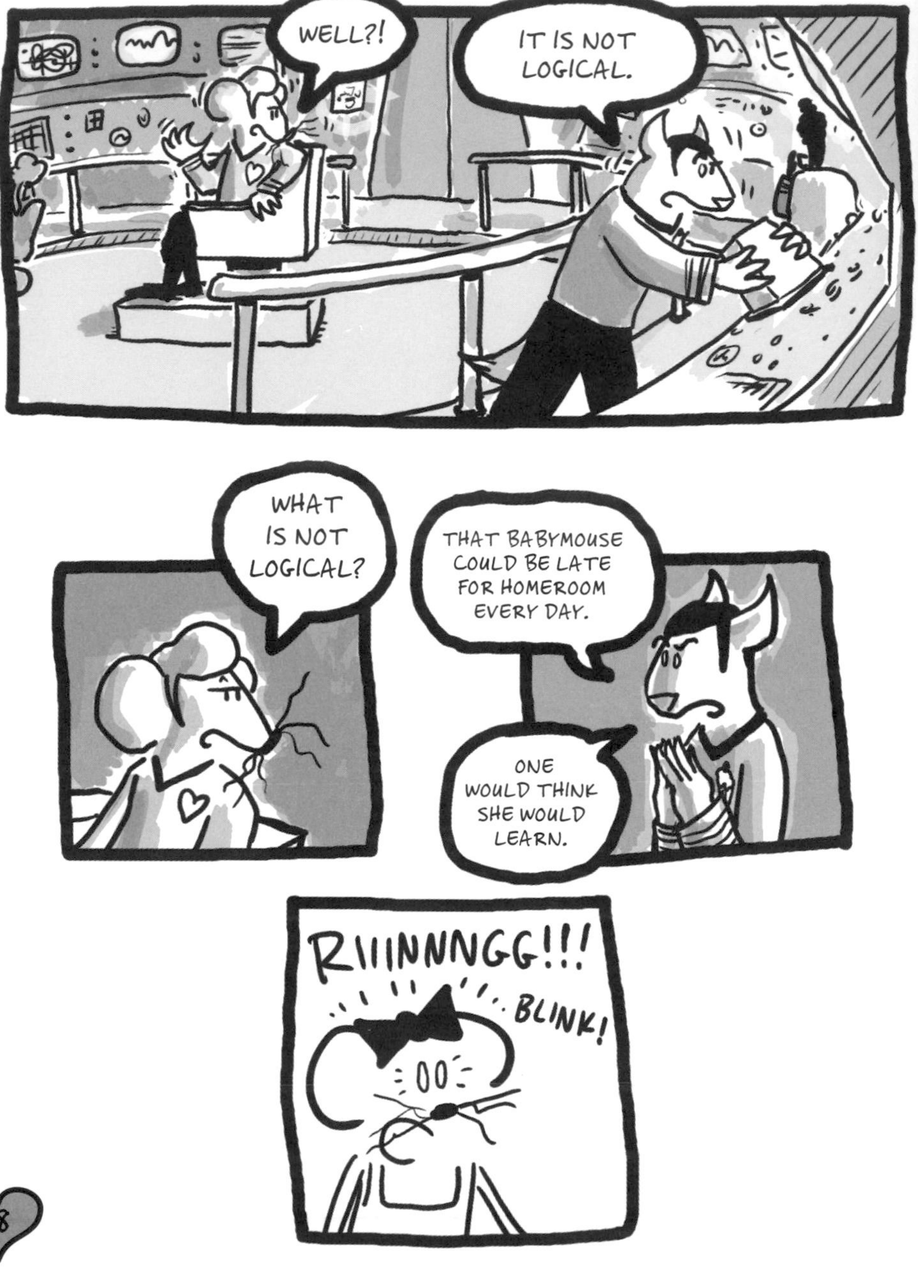
WELL?!
IT IS NOT LOGICAL.
WHAT IS NOT LOGICAL?
THAT BABYMOUSE COULD BE LATE FOR HOMEROOM EVERY DAY.
ONE WOULD THINK SHE WOULD LEARN.
RIIINNNGG!!!
BLINK!

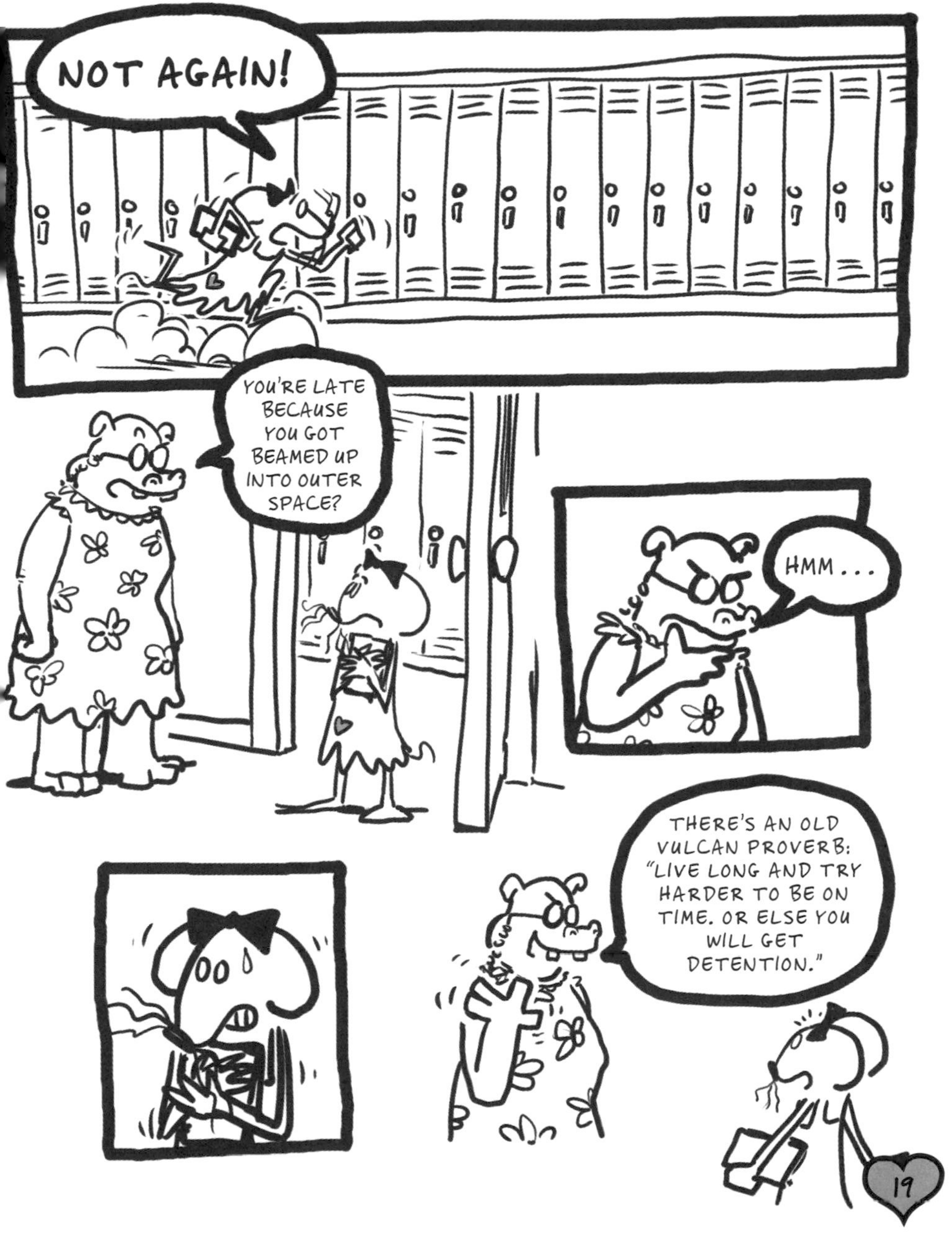
NOT AGAIN!
YOU'RE LATE BECAUSE YOU GOT BEAMED UP INTO OUTER SPACE?
HMM . . .
THERE'S AN OLD VULCAN PROVERB: "LIVE LONG AND TRY HARDER TO BE ON TIME. OR ELSE YOU WILL GET DETENTION."

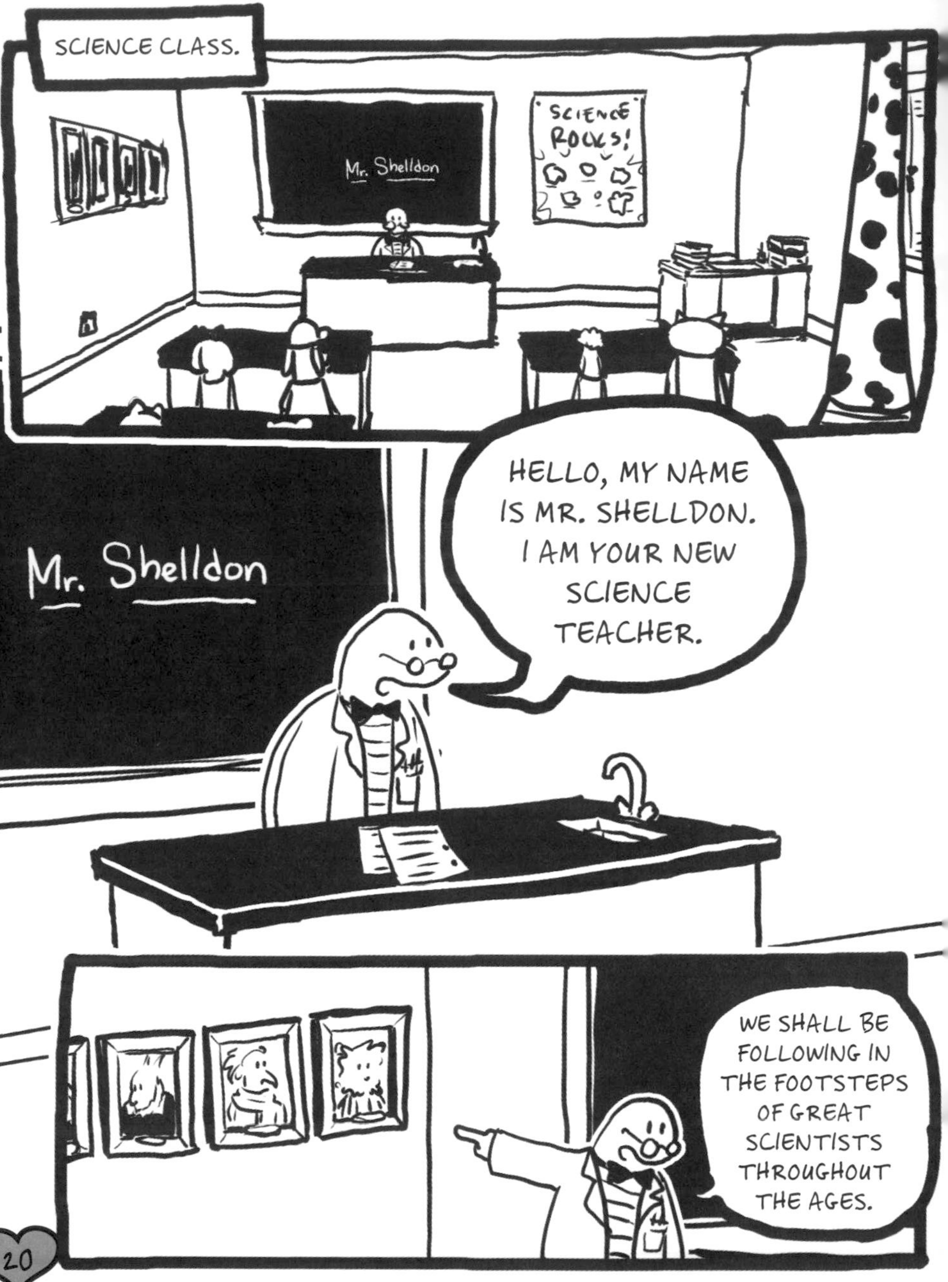
SCIENCE CLASS.
Mr. Shelldon
SCIENCE ROCKS!
Mr. Shelldon
HELLO, MY NAME IS MR. SHELLDON. I AM YOUR NEW SCIENCE TEACHER.
WE SHALL BE FOLLOWING IN THE FOOTSTEPS OF GREAT SCIENTISTS THROUGHOUT THE AGES.

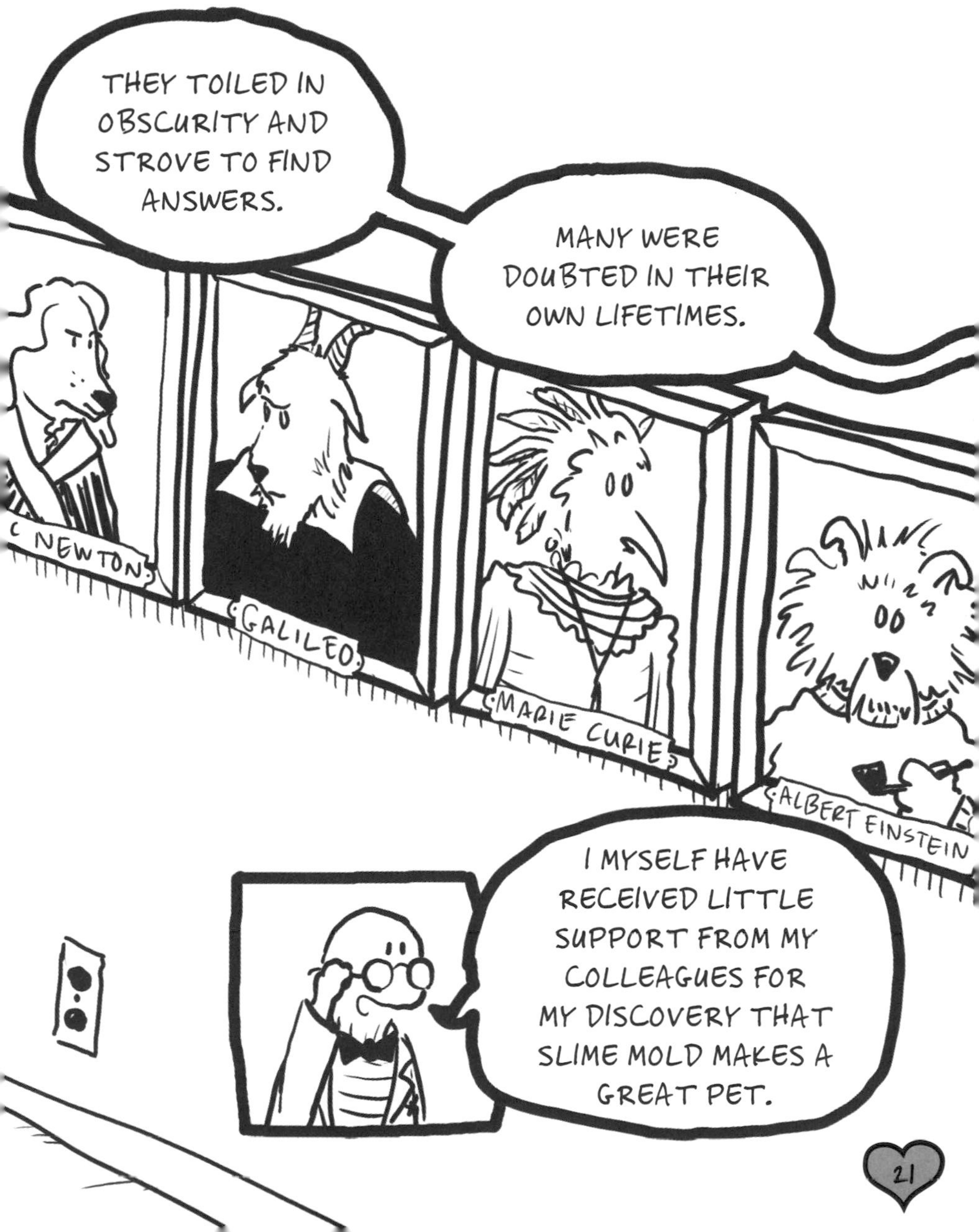
THEY TOILED IN OBSCURITY AND STROVE TO FIND ANSWERS.
MANY WERE DOUBTED IN THEIR OWN LIFETIMES.
NEWTON
GALILEO
MARIE CURIE
ALBERT EINSTEIN
I MYSELF HAVE RECEIVED LITTLE SUPPORT FROM MY COLLEAGUES FOR MY DISCOVERY THAT SLIME MOLD MAKES A GREAT PET.

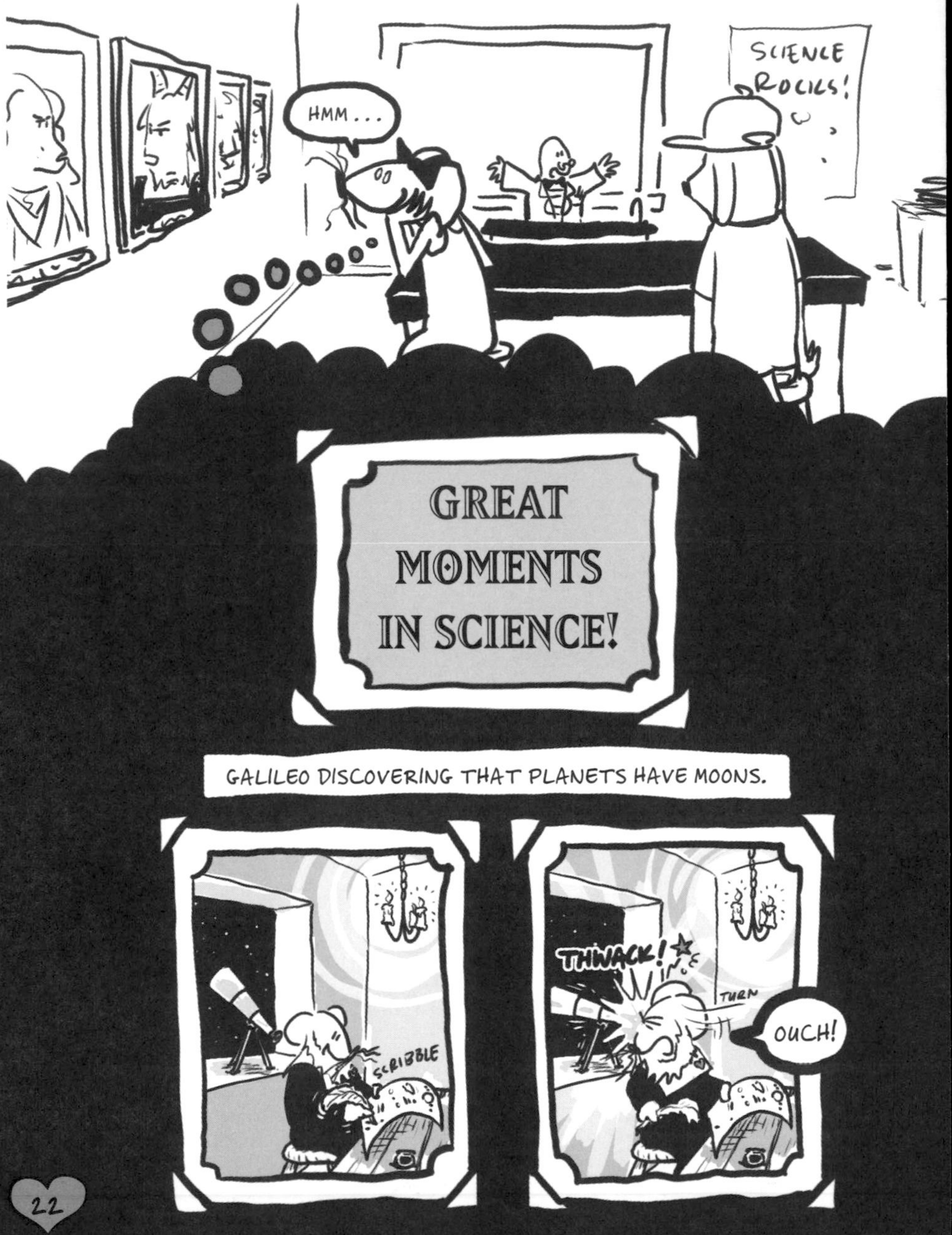

SCIENCE ROCKS!
HMM...
GREAT MOMENTS IN SCIENCE!
GALILEO DISCOVERING THAT PLANETS HAVE MOONS.
SCRIBBLE
THWACK!
TURN
OUCH!

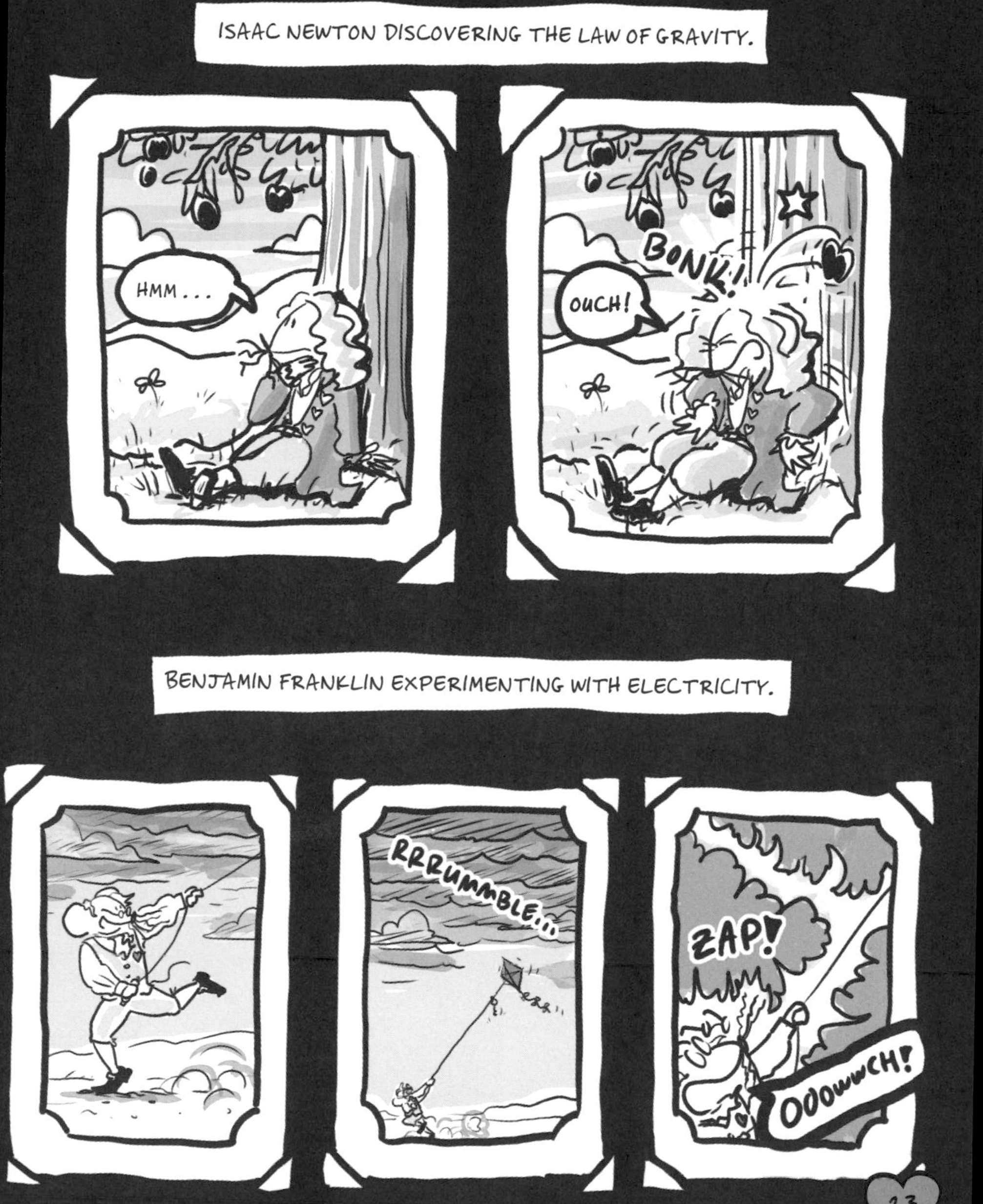
ISAAC NEWTON DISCOVERING THE LAW OF GRAVITY.
HMM...
BONK!
OUCH!
BENJAMIN FRANKLIN EXPERIMENTING WITH ELECTRICITY.
RRRUMMBLE...
ZAP!
OOOWWCH!

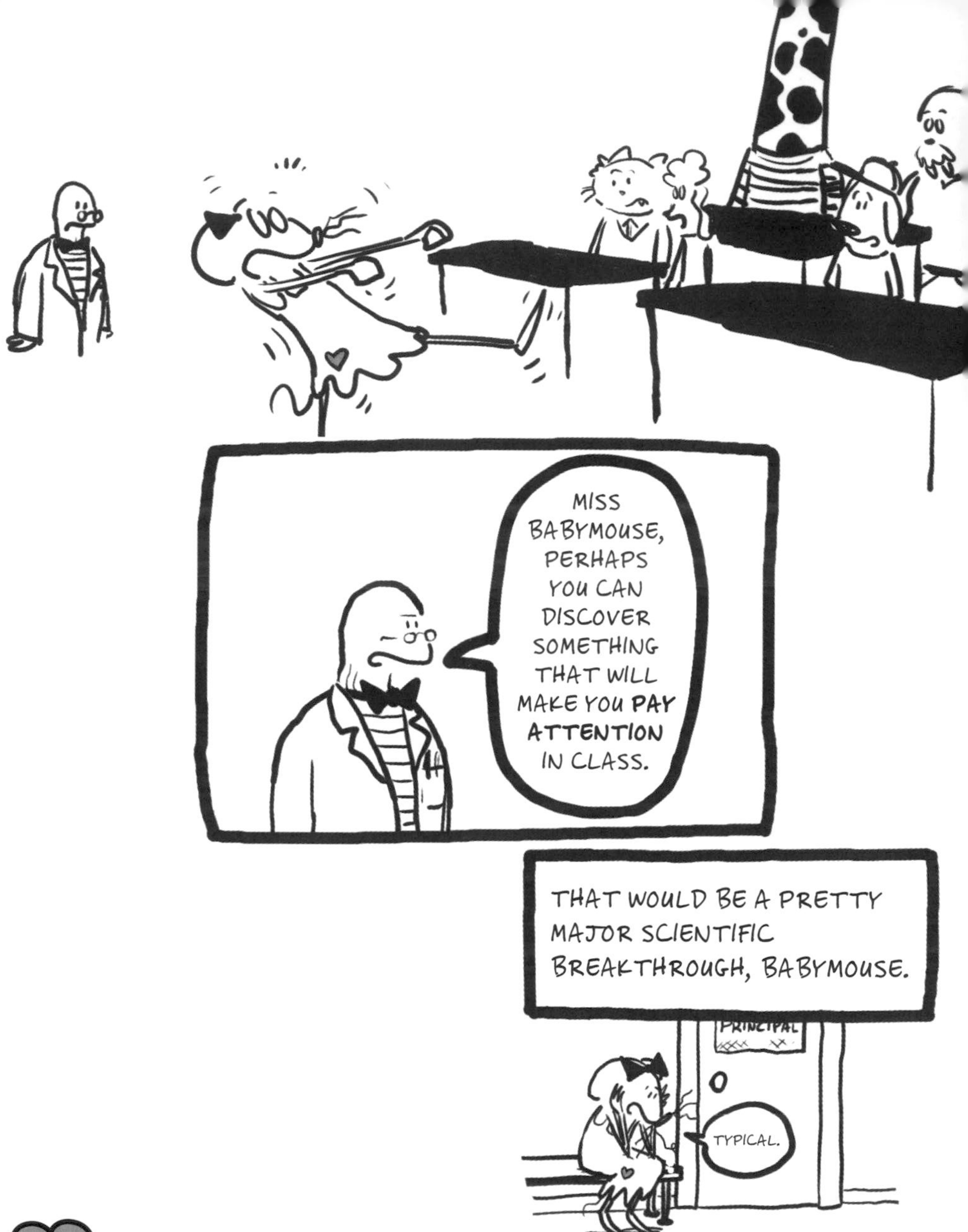
MISS BABYMOUSE, PERHAPS YOU CAN DISCOVER SOMETHING THAT WILL MAKE YOU **PAY ATTENTION** IN CLASS.
THAT WOULD BE A PRETTY MAJOR SCIENTIFIC BREAKTHROUGH, BABYMOUSE.
PRINCIPAL
TYPICAL.

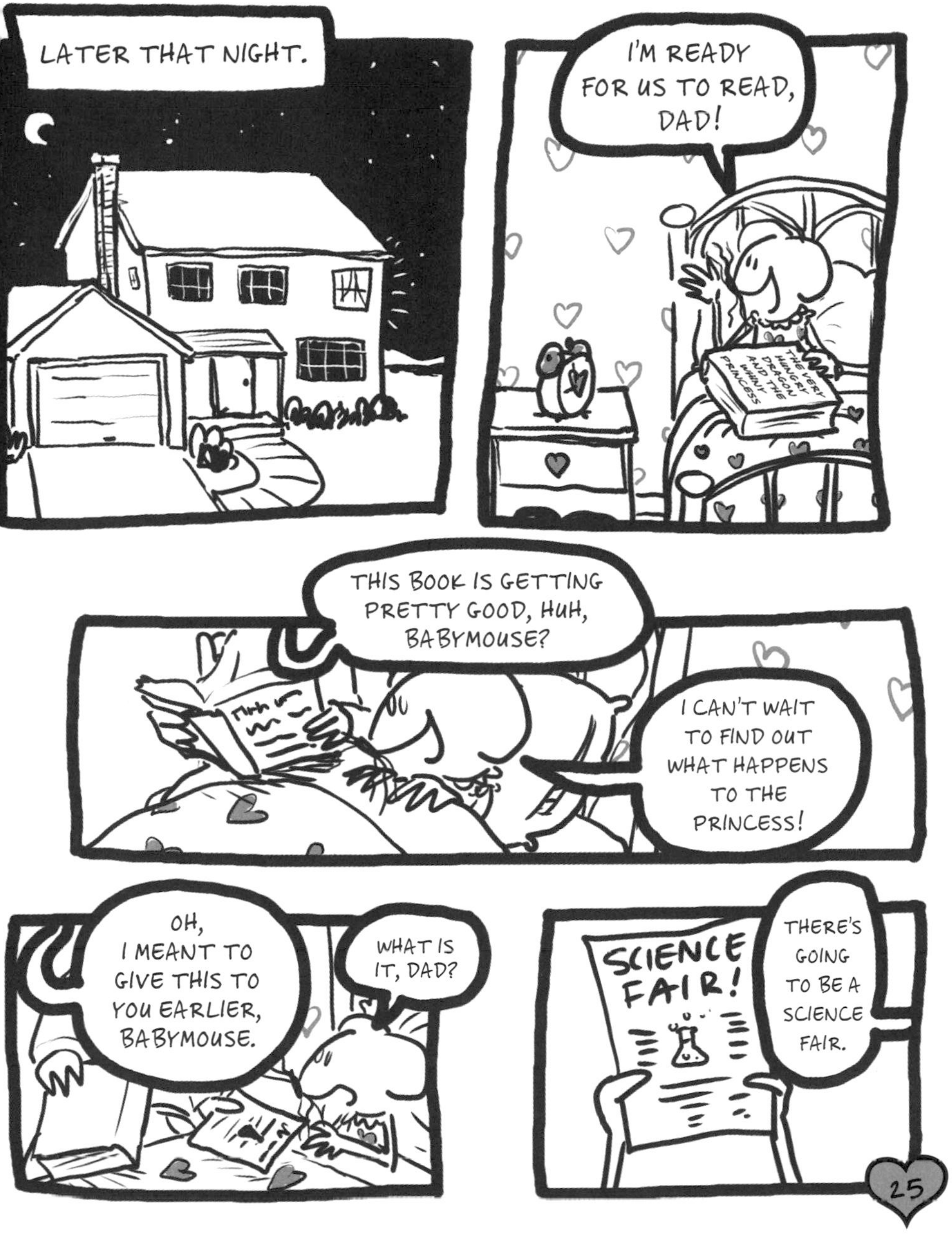
LATER THAT NIGHT.
I'M READY FOR US TO READ, DAD!
THE VERY HUNGRY DRAGON AND THE WHINY PRINCESS
THIS BOOK IS GETTING PRETTY GOOD, HUH, BABYMOUSE?
I CAN'T WAIT TO FIND OUT WHAT HAPPENS TO THE PRINCESS!
OH, I MEANT TO GIVE THIS TO YOU EARLIER, BABYMOUSE.
WHAT IS IT, DAD?
SCIENCE FAIR!
THERE'S GOING TO BE A SCIENCE FAIR.

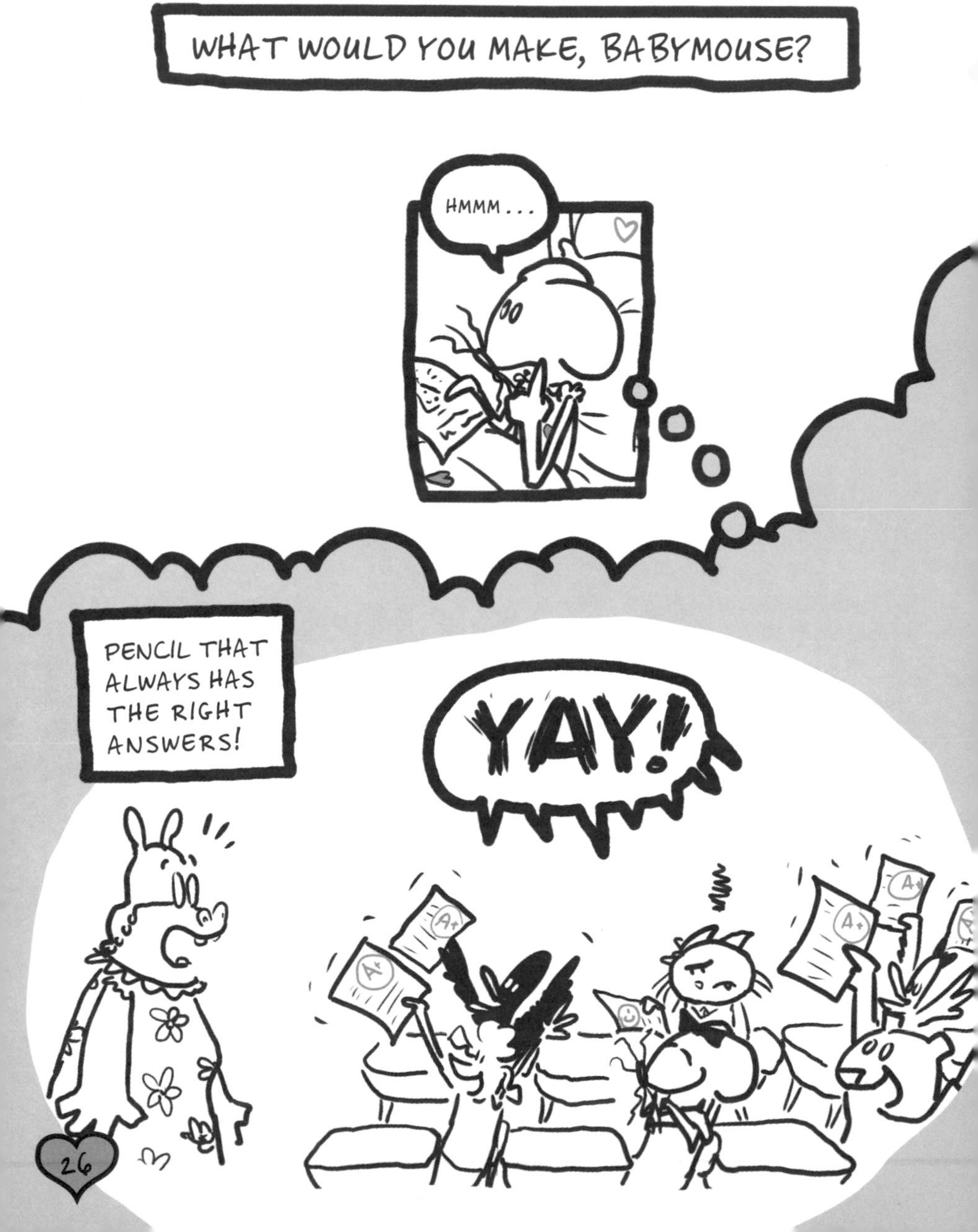
WHAT WOULD YOU MAKE, BABYMOUSE?
HMMM...
PENCIL THAT ALWAYS HAS THE RIGHT ANSWERS!
YAY!

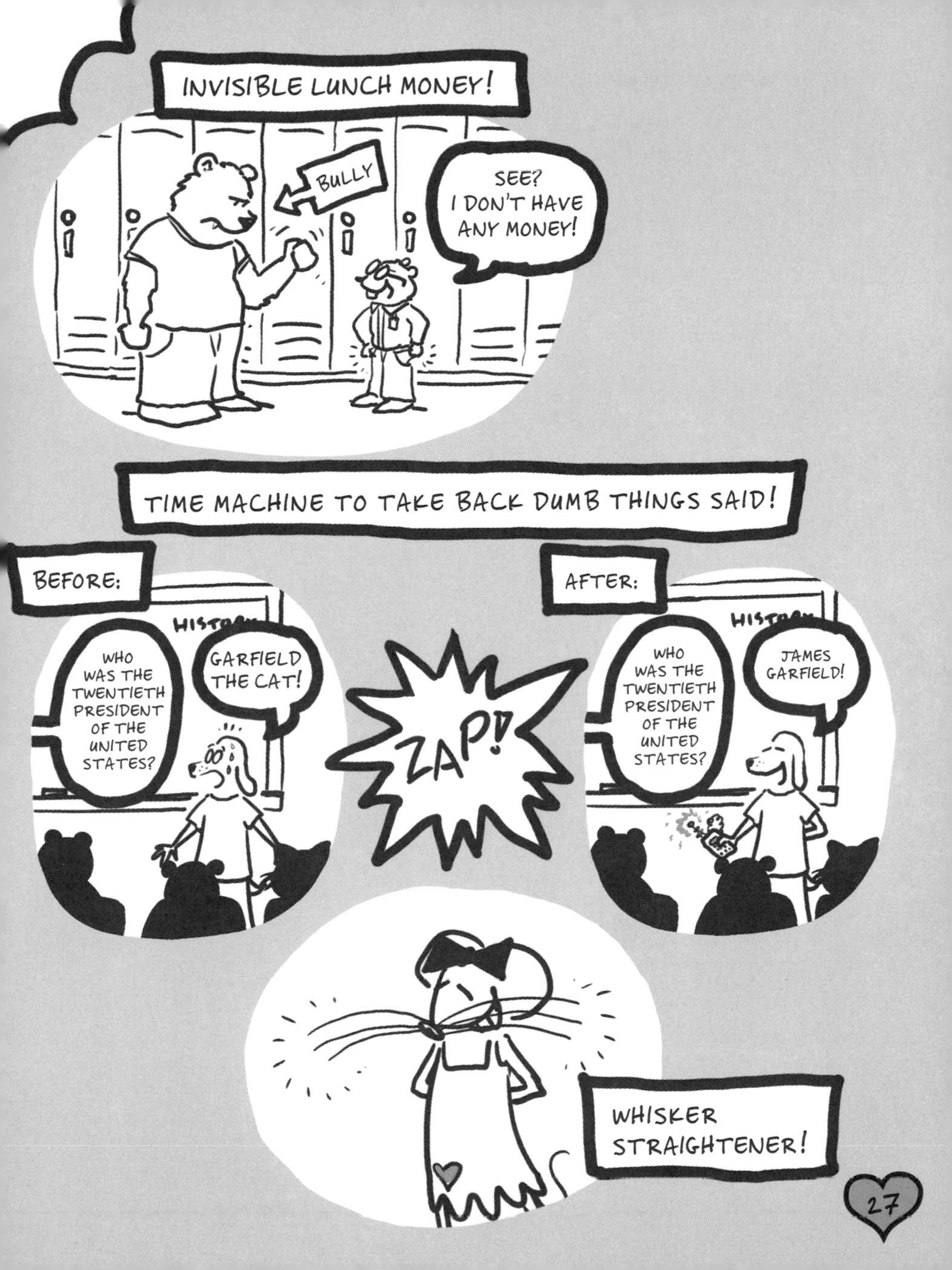

INVISIBLE LUNCH MONEY!
BULLY
SEE? I DON'T HAVE ANY MONEY!
TIME MACHINE TO TAKE BACK DUMB THINGS SAID!
BEFORE:
HISTORY
WHO WAS THE TWENTIETH PRESIDENT OF THE UNITED STATES?
GARFIELD THE CAT!
ZAP!
AFTER:
WHO WAS THE TWENTIETH PRESIDENT OF THE UNITED STATES?
JAMES GARFIELD!
WHISKER STRAIGHTENER!

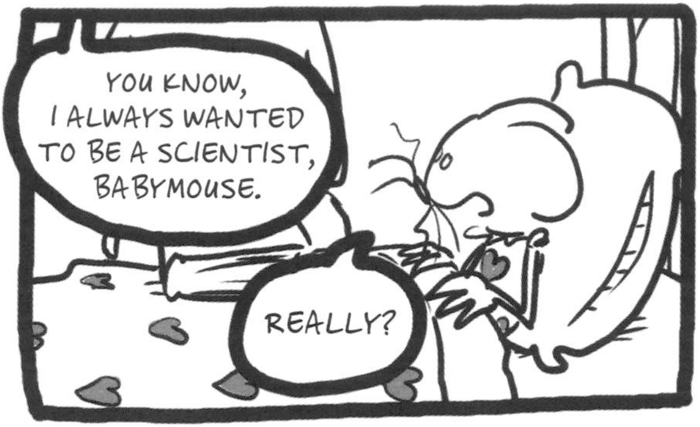
YOU KNOW, I ALWAYS WANTED TO BE A SCIENTIST, BABYMOUSE.
REALLY?

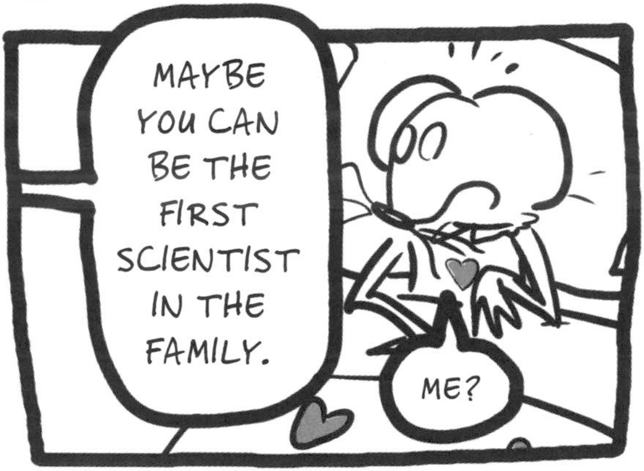
MAYBE YOU CAN BE THE FIRST SCIENTIST IN THE FAMILY.
ME?

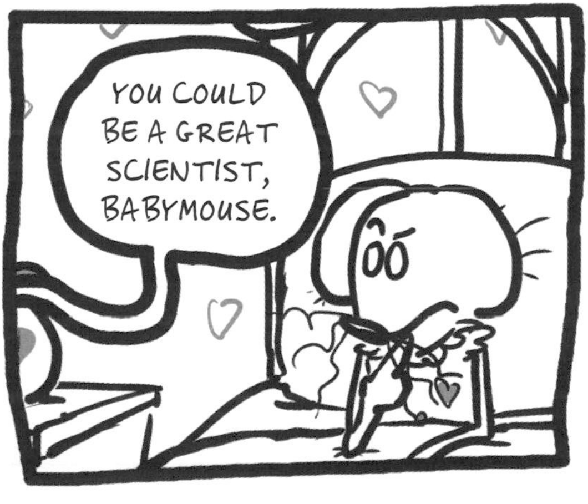
YOU COULD BE A GREAT SCIENTIST, BABYMOUSE.

GREAT DISCOVERIES OF DR. BABYMOUSE!

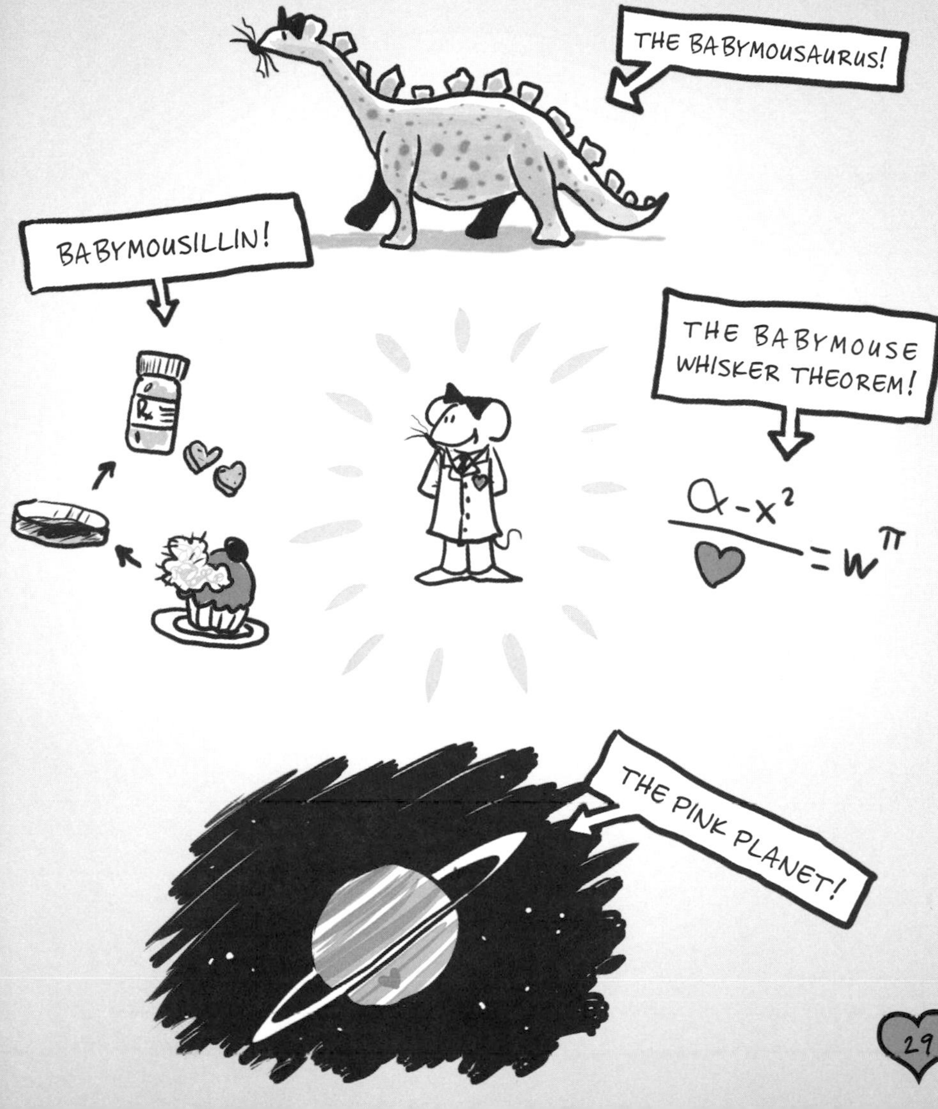
THE BABYMOUSAURUS!
BABYMOUSILLIN!
THE BABYMOUSE WHISKER THEOREM!
$\frac{\alpha - x^2}{\heartsuit} = w^{\pi}$
THE PINK PLANET!

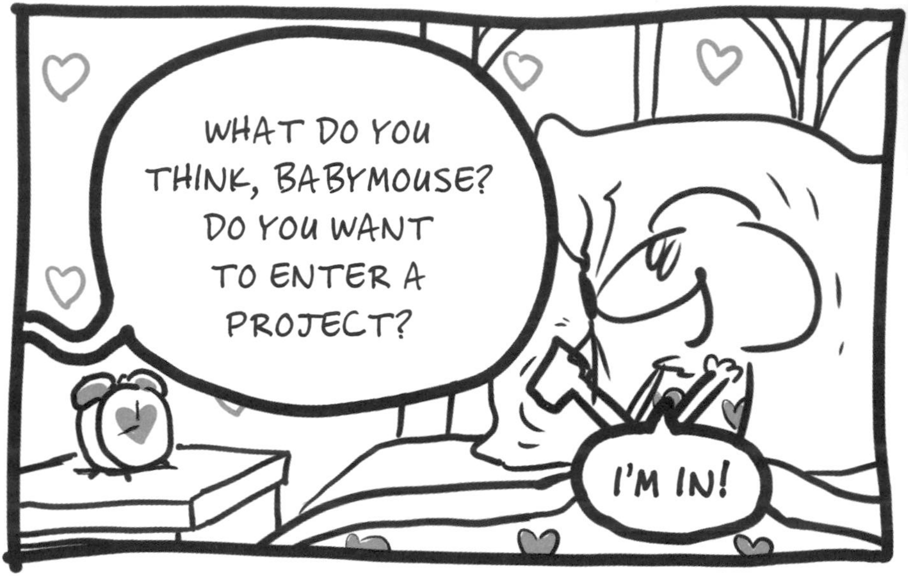
WHAT DO YOU THINK, BABYMOUSE? DO YOU WANT TO ENTER A PROJECT?
I'M IN!

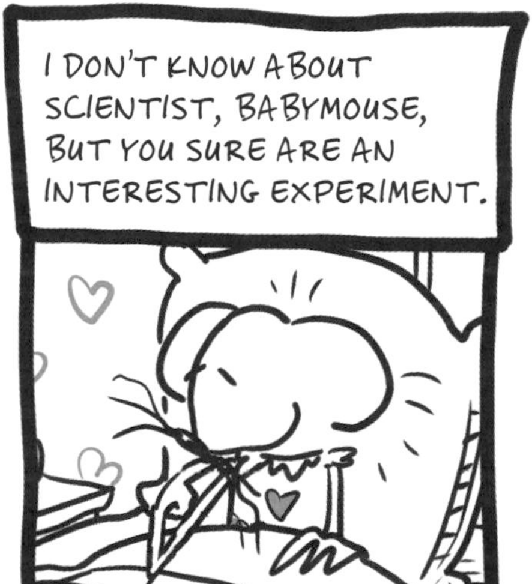
I DON'T KNOW ABOUT SCIENTIST, BABYMOUSE, BUT YOU SURE ARE AN INTERESTING EXPERIMENT.

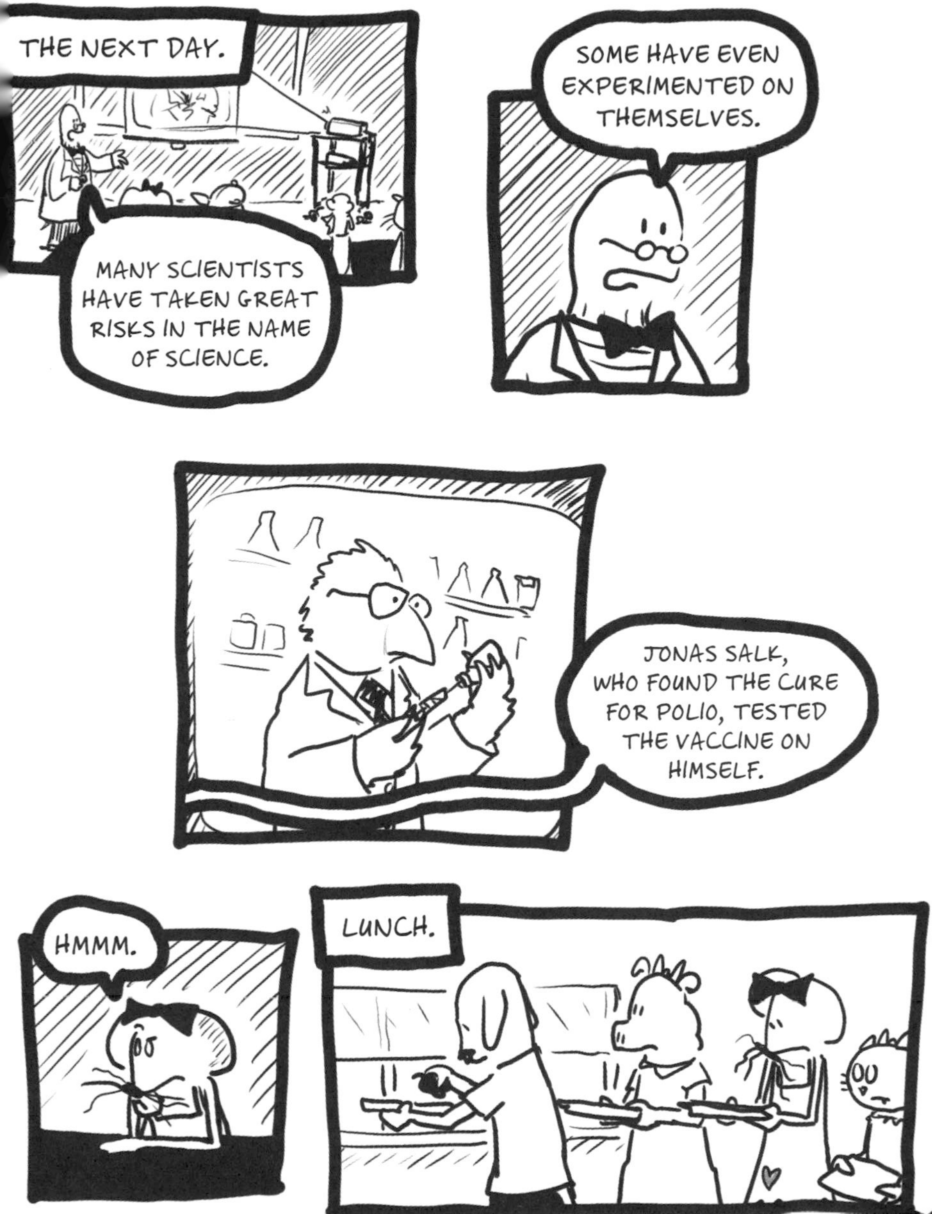
THE NEXT DAY.
MANY SCIENTISTS HAVE TAKEN GREAT RISKS IN THE NAME OF SCIENCE.
SOME HAVE EVEN EXPERIMENTED ON THEMSELVES.
JONAS SALK, WHO FOUND THE CURE FOR POLIO, TESTED THE VACCINE ON HIMSELF.
HMMM.
LUNCH.

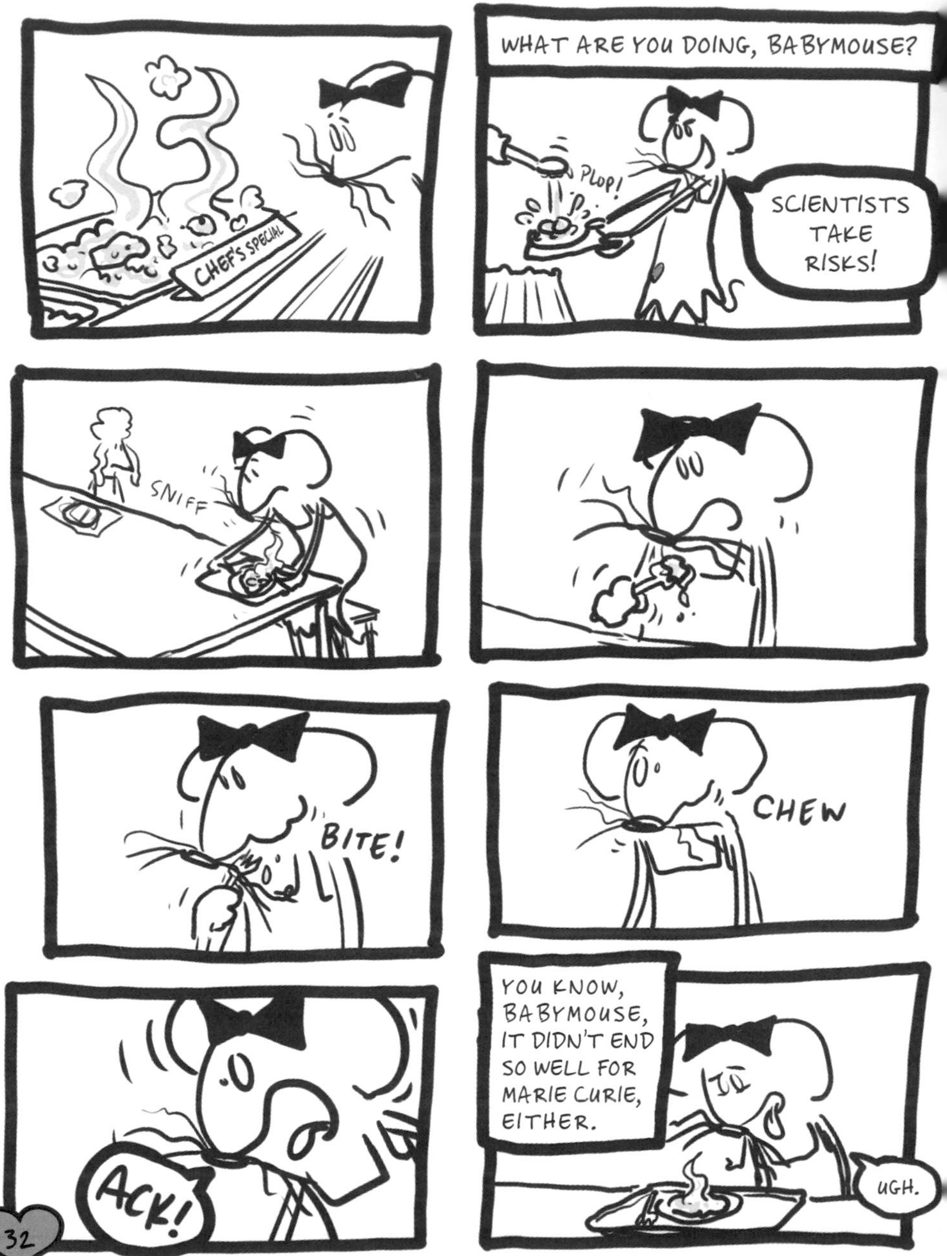
CHEF'S SPECIAL
WHAT ARE YOU DOING, BABYMOUSE?
PLOP!
SCIENTISTS TAKE RISKS!
SNIFF
BITE!
CHEW
ACK!
YOU KNOW, BABYMOUSE, IT DIDN'T END SO WELL FOR MARIE CURIE, EITHER.
UGH.

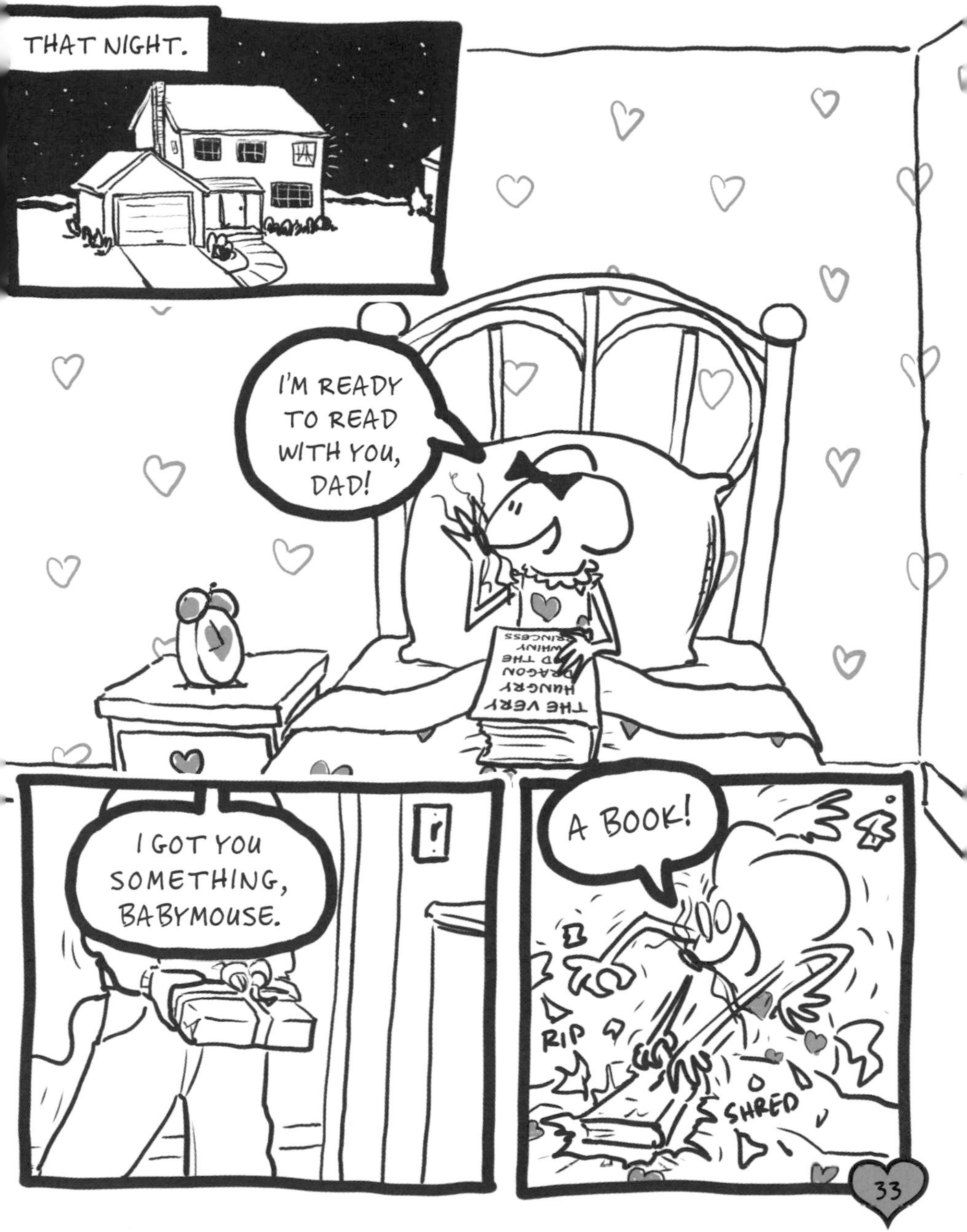
THAT NIGHT.
I'M READY TO READ WITH YOU, DAD!
I GOT YOU SOMETHING, BABYMOUSE.
A BOOK!
RIP
SHRED

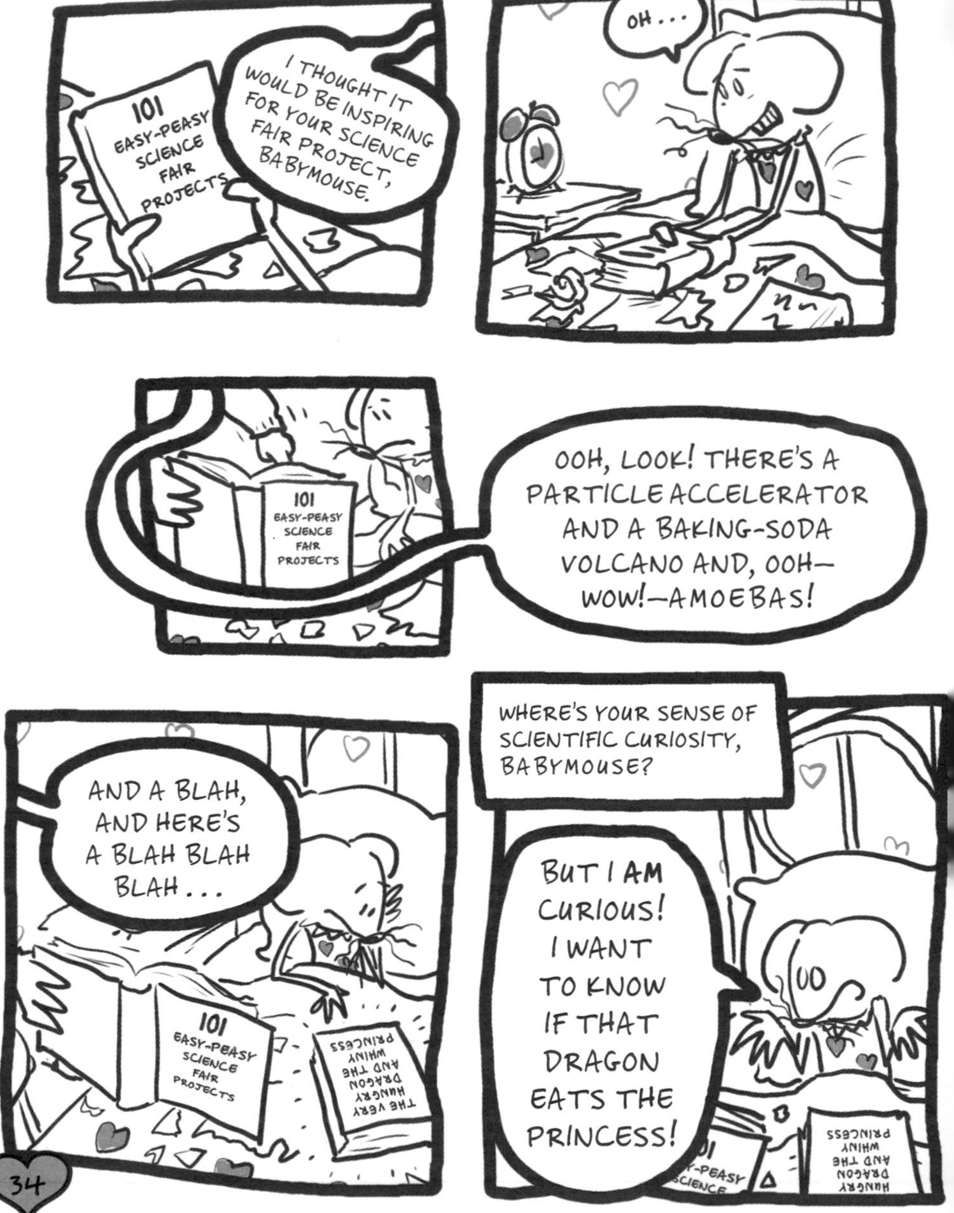
I THOUGHT IT WOULD BE INSPIRING FOR YOUR SCIENCE FAIR PROJECT, BABYMOUSE.
101 EASY-PEASY SCIENCE FAIR PROJECTS
OH . . .
OOH, LOOK! THERE'S A PARTICLE ACCELERATOR AND A BAKING-SODA VOLCANO AND, OOH—WOW!—AMOEBAS!
101 EASY-PEASY SCIENCE FAIR PROJECTS
AND A BLAH, AND HERE'S A BLAH BLAH BLAH . . .
101 EASY-PEASY SCIENCE FAIR PROJECTS
THE VERY HUNGRY DRAGON AND THE WHINY PRINCESS
WHERE'S YOUR SENSE OF SCIENTIFIC CURIOSITY, BABYMOUSE?
BUT I AM CURIOUS! I WANT TO KNOW IF THAT DRAGON EATS THE PRINCESS!

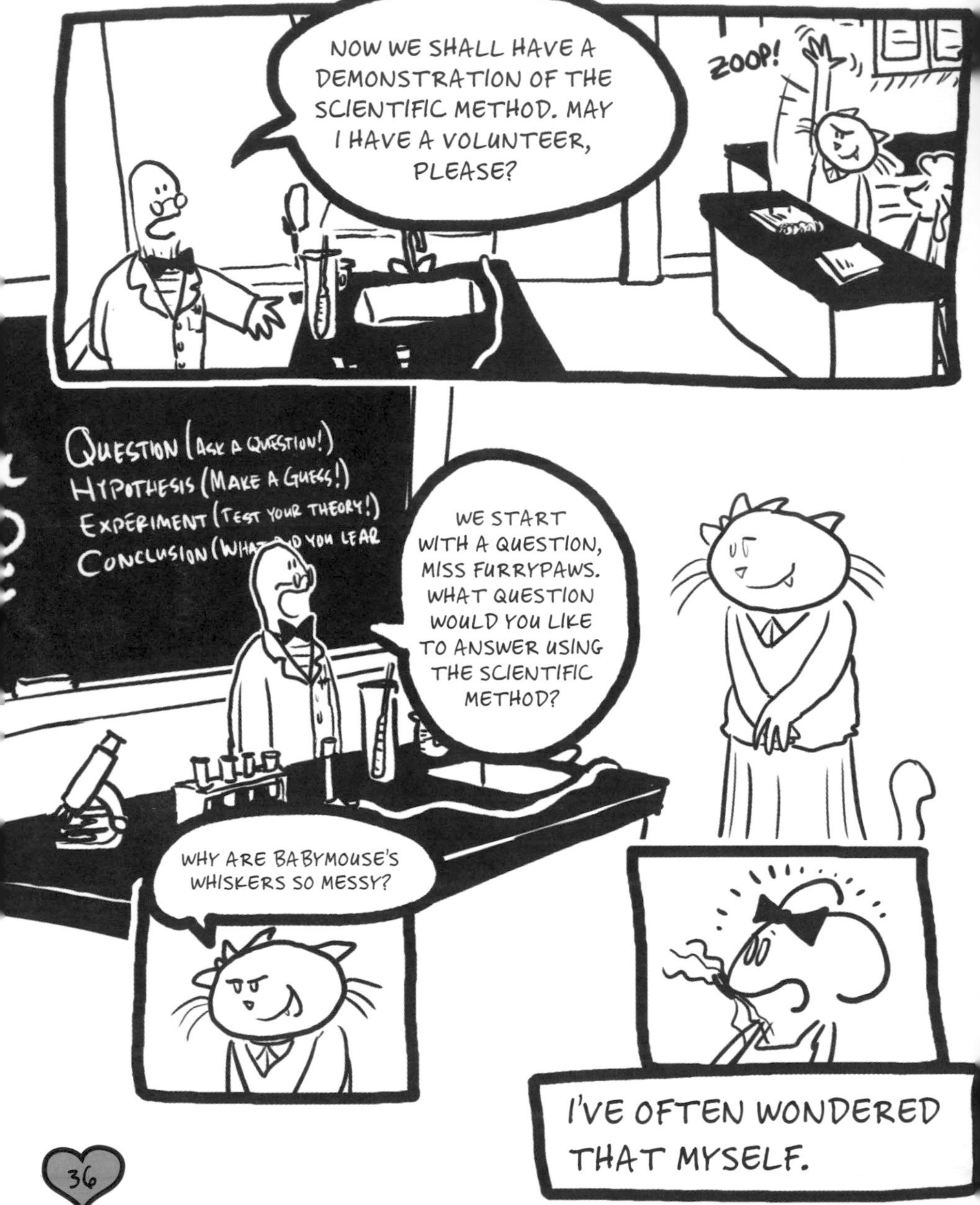

NOW WE SHALL HAVE A DEMONSTRATION OF THE SCIENTIFIC METHOD. MAY I HAVE A VOLUNTEER, PLEASE?
ZOOP!
QUESTION (ASK A QUESTION!)
HYPOTHESIS (MAKE A GUESS!)
EXPERIMENT (TEST YOUR THEORY!)
CONCLUSION (WHA
YOU LEAR
WE START WITH A QUESTION, MISS FURRYPAWS. WHAT QUESTION WOULD YOU LIKE TO ANSWER USING THE SCIENTIFIC METHOD?
WHY ARE BABYMOUSE'S WHISKERS SO MESSY?
I'VE OFTEN WONDERED THAT MYSELF.

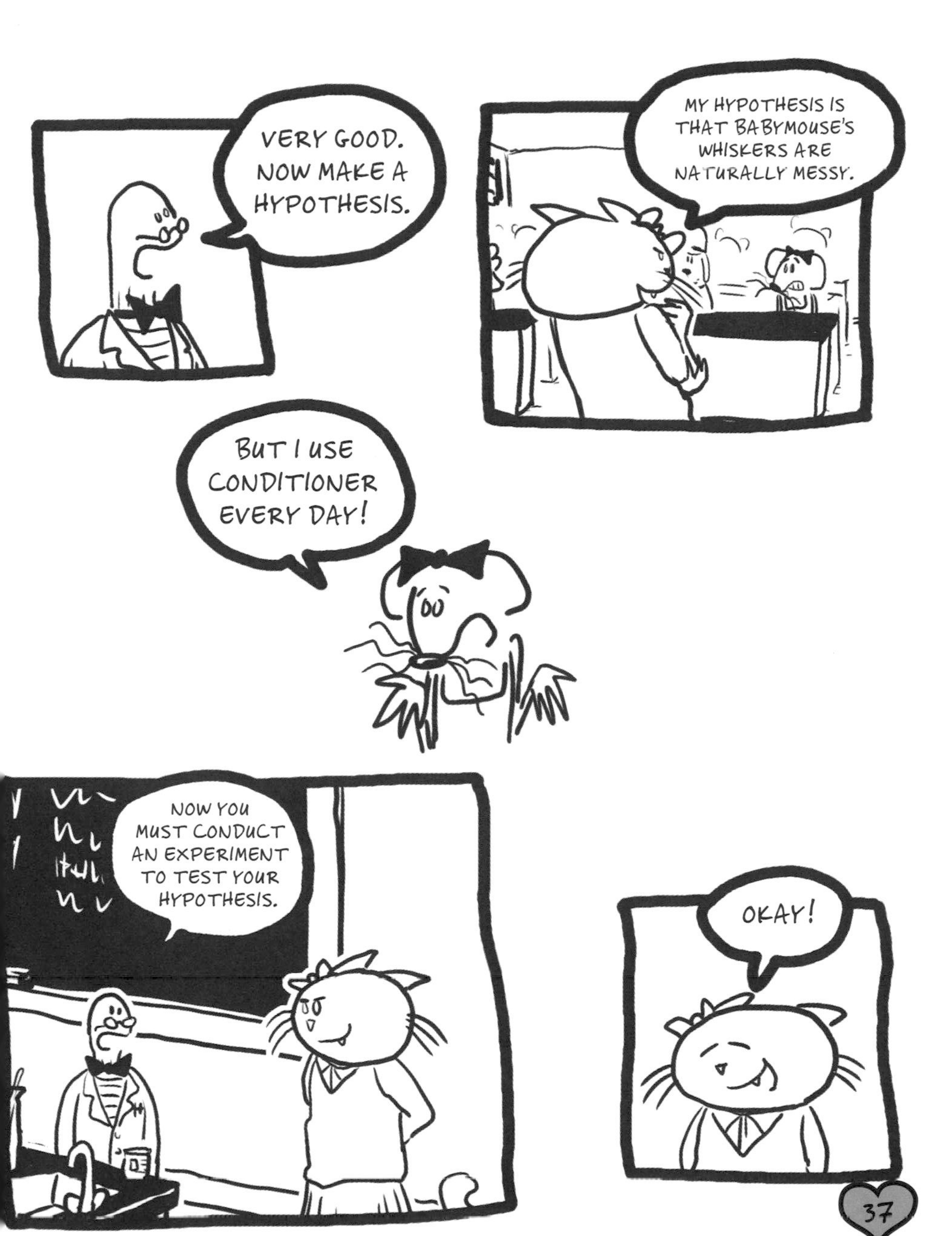

VERY GOOD. NOW MAKE A HYPOTHESIS.
MY HYPOTHESIS IS THAT BABYMOUSE'S WHISKERS ARE NATURALLY MESSY.
BUT I USE CONDITIONER EVERY DAY!
NOW YOU MUST CONDUCT AN EXPERIMENT TO TEST YOUR HYPOTHESIS.
OKAY!

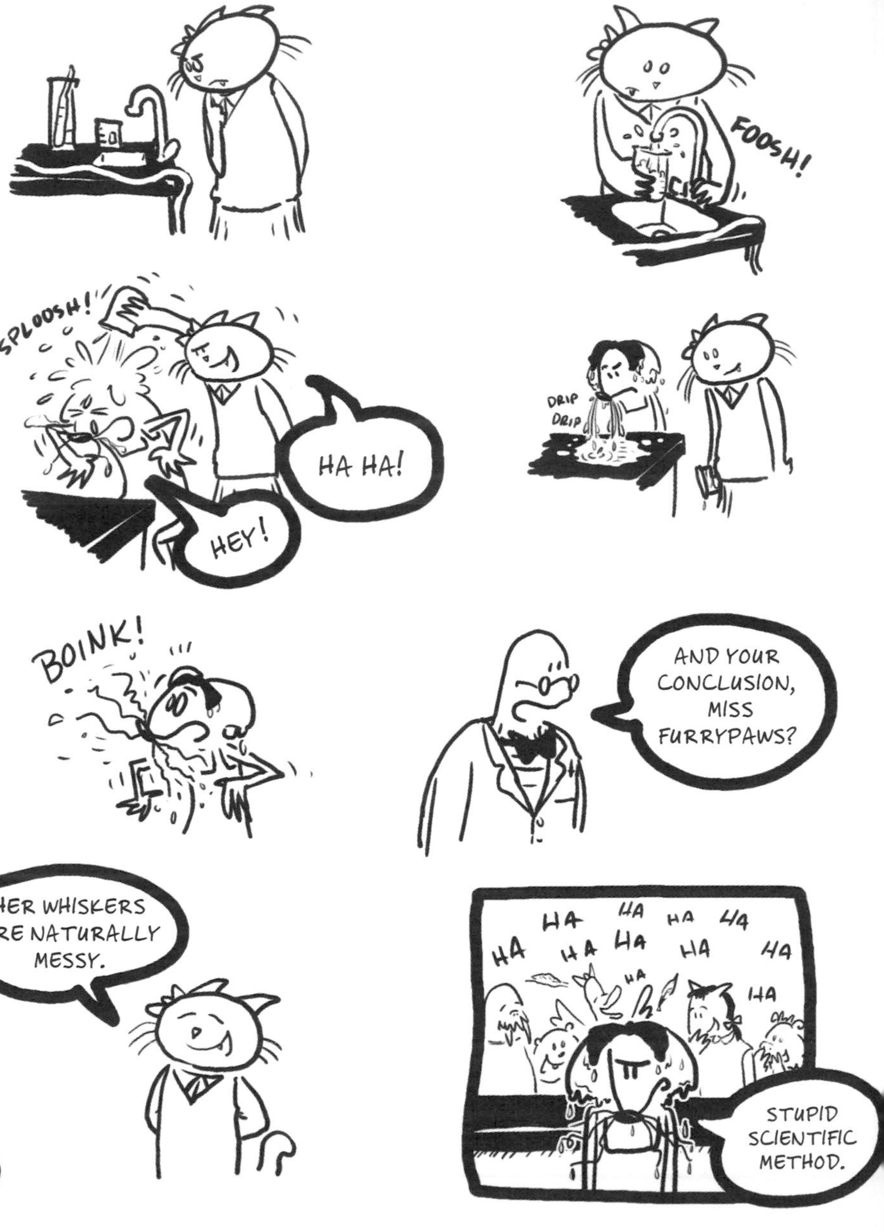
FOOSH!
SPLOOSH!
HA HA!
HEY!
DRIP
DRIP
BOINK!
AND YOUR CONCLUSION, MISS FURRYPAWS?
HER WHISKERS ARE NATURALLY MESSY.
HA HA HA HA HA HA HA HA HA HA HA HA
STUPID SCIENTIFIC METHOD.

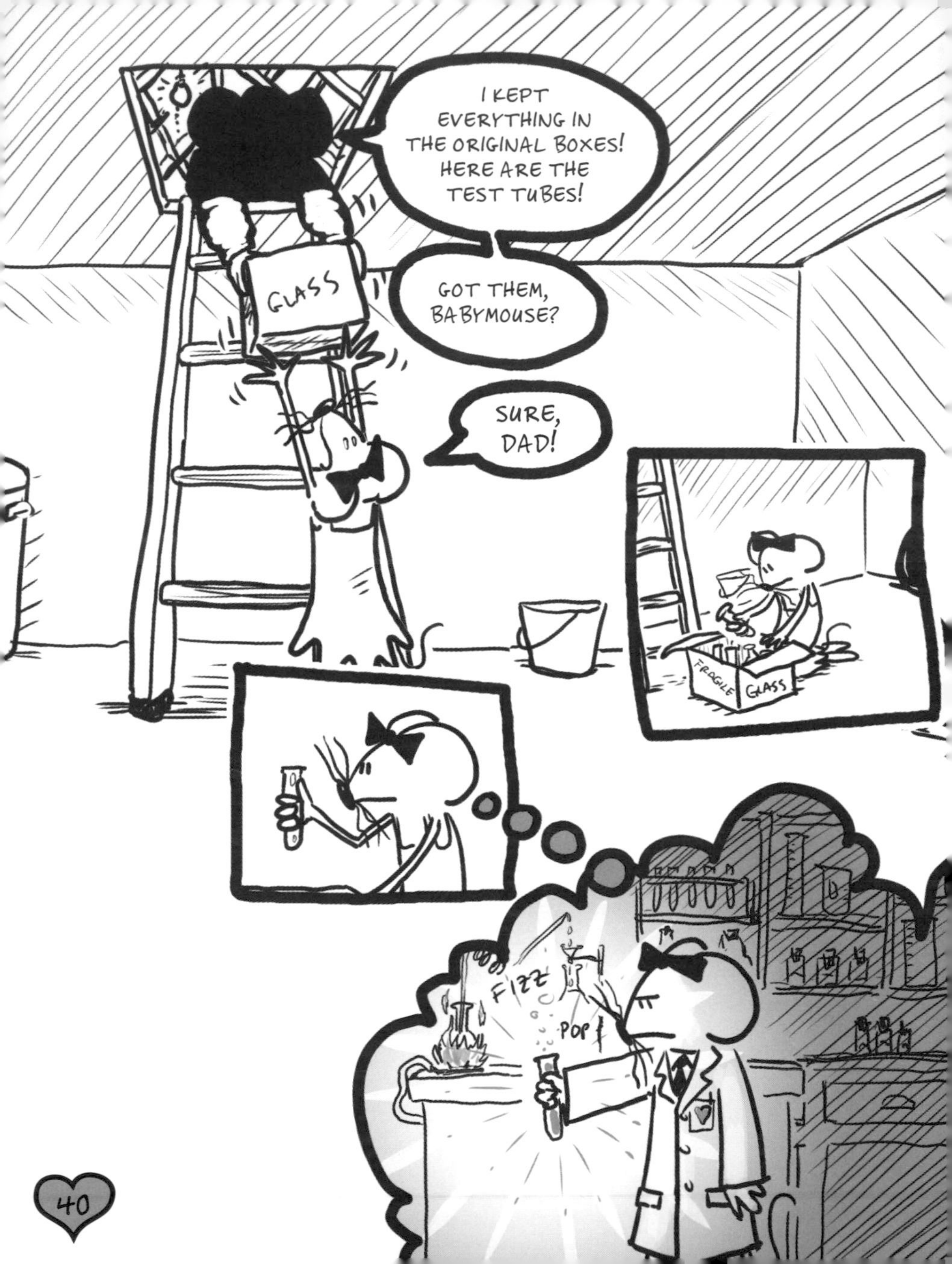
I KEPT EVERYTHING IN THE ORIGINAL BOXES! HERE ARE THE TEST TUBES!
GLASS
GOT THEM, BABYMOUSE?
SURE, DAD!
FRAGILE
GLASS
FIZZ
POP

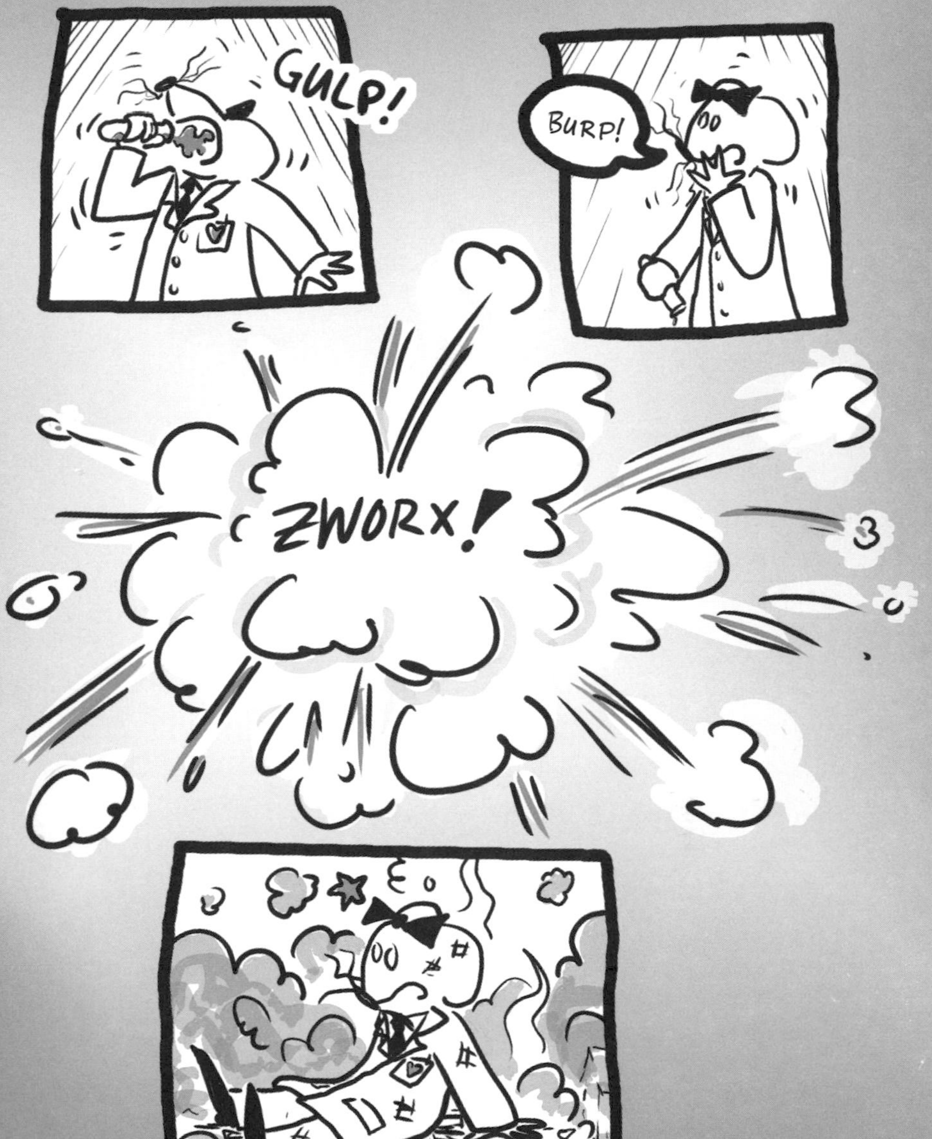
GULP!
BURP!
ZWORX!

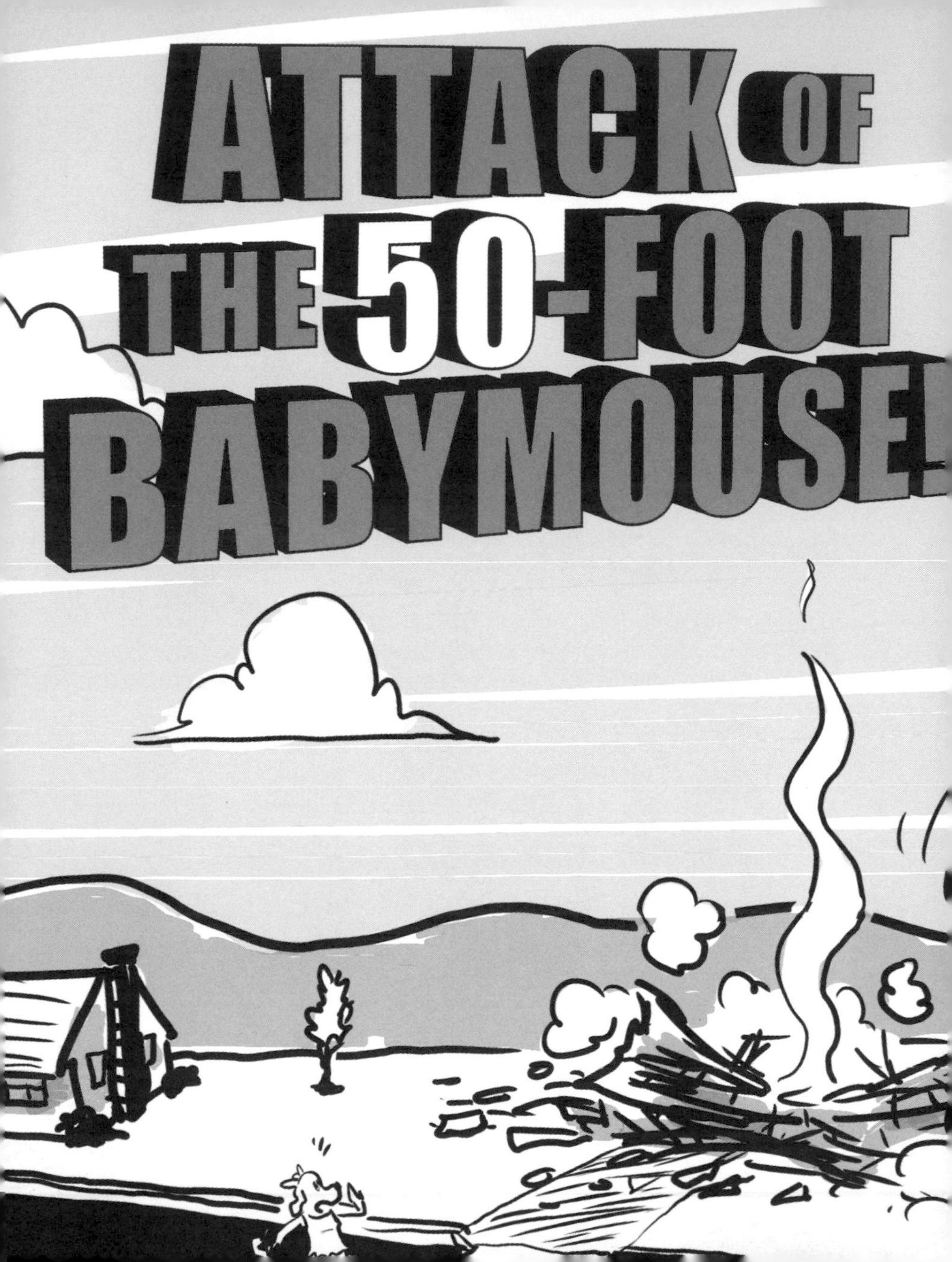
ATTACK OF
THE 50-FOOT
BABYMOUSE!

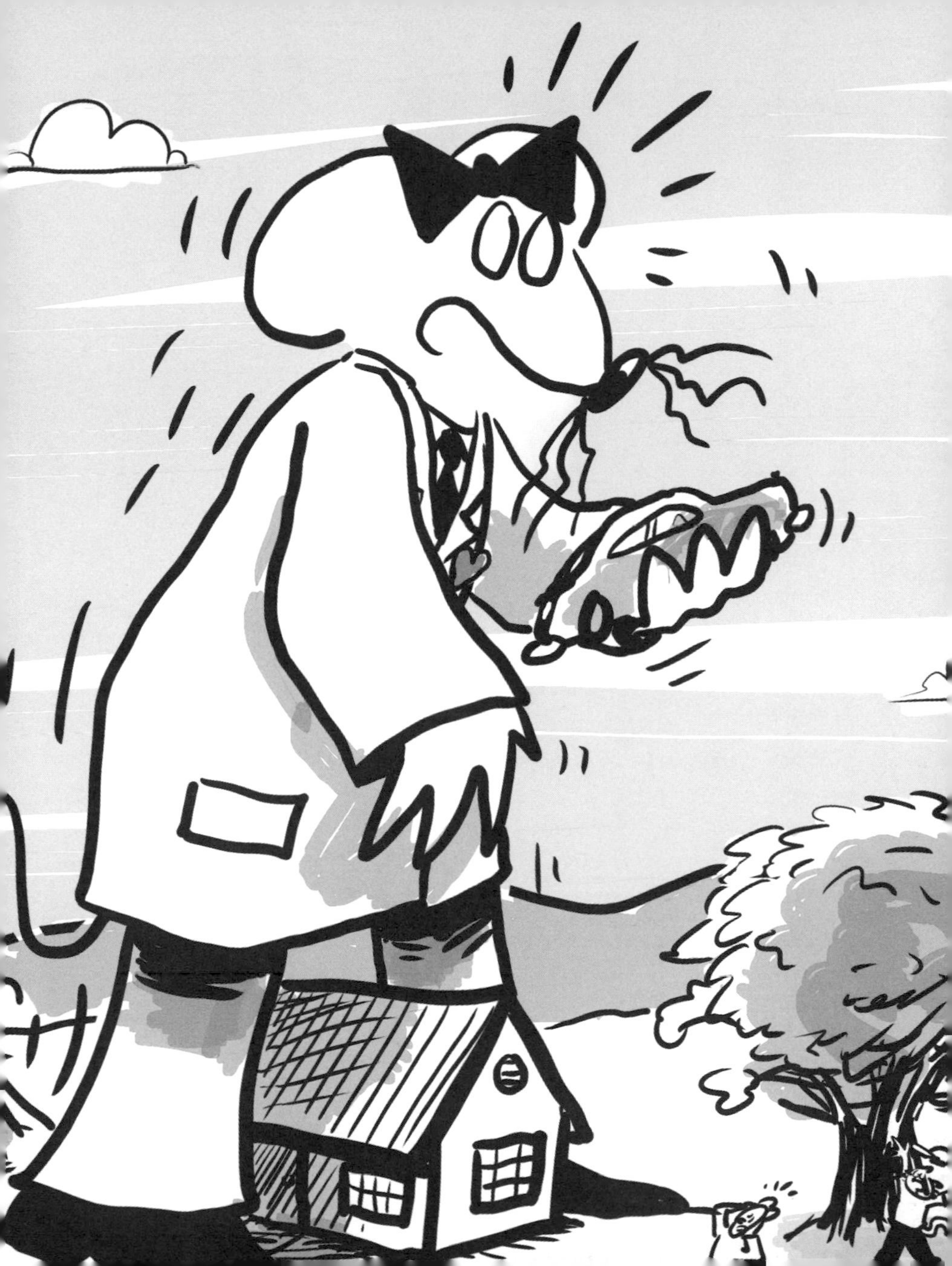

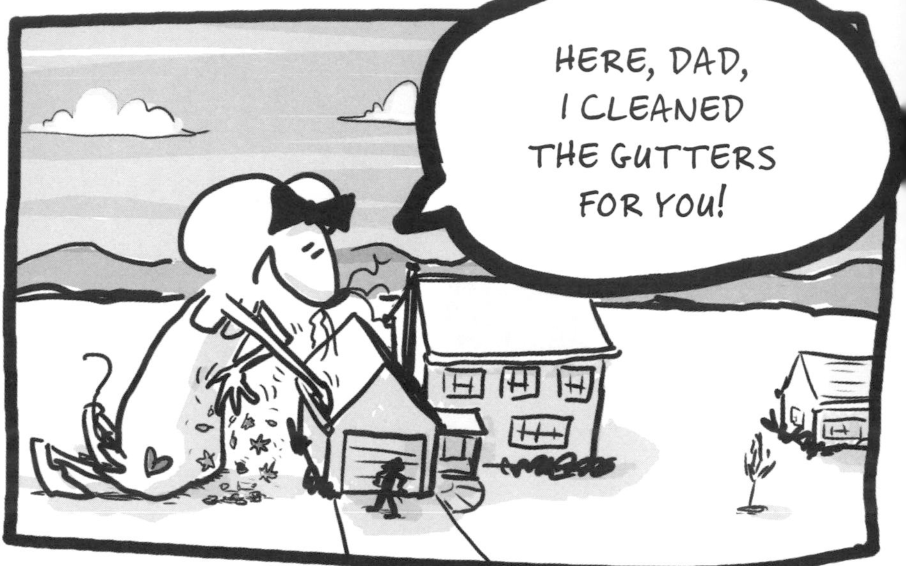
HERE, DAD, I CLEANED THE GUTTERS FOR YOU!

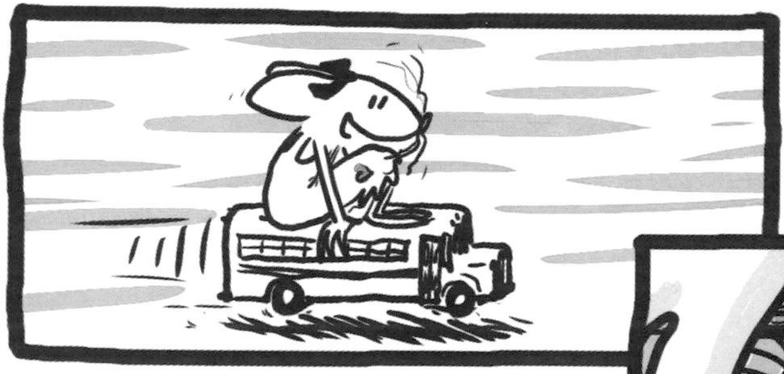

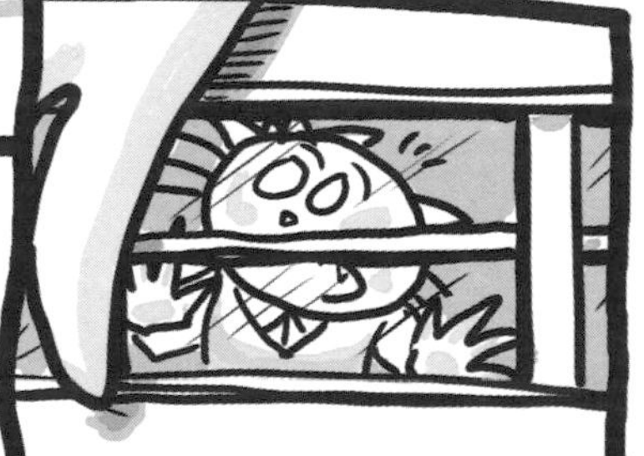

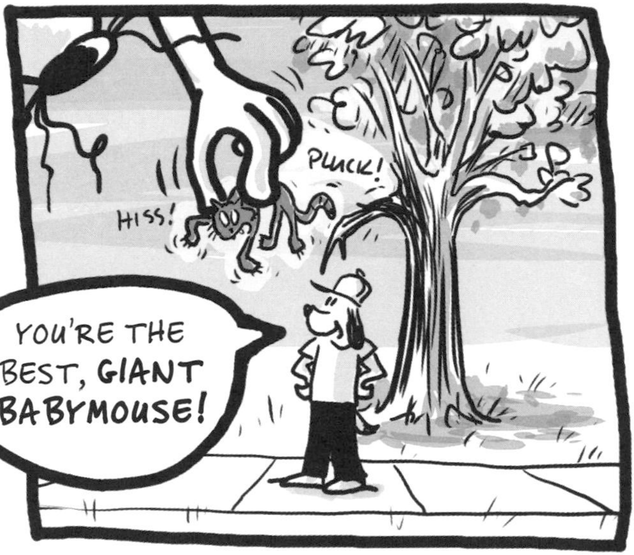
PLUCK!
HISS!
YOU'RE THE BEST, **GIANT BABYMOUSE!**

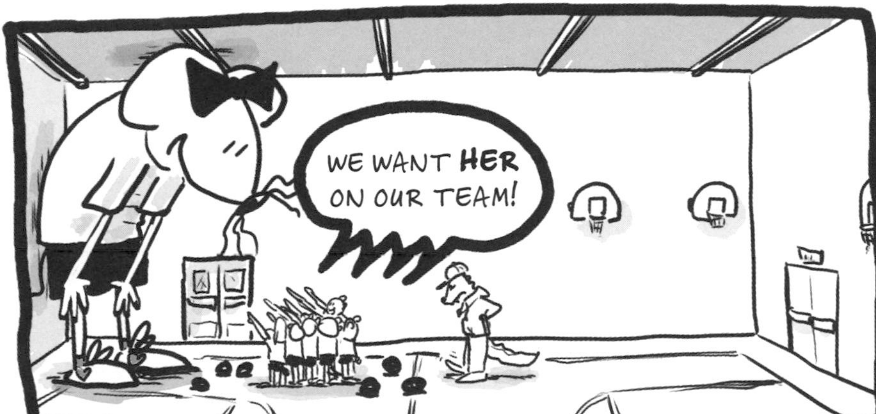
WE WANT **HER** ON OUR TEAM!

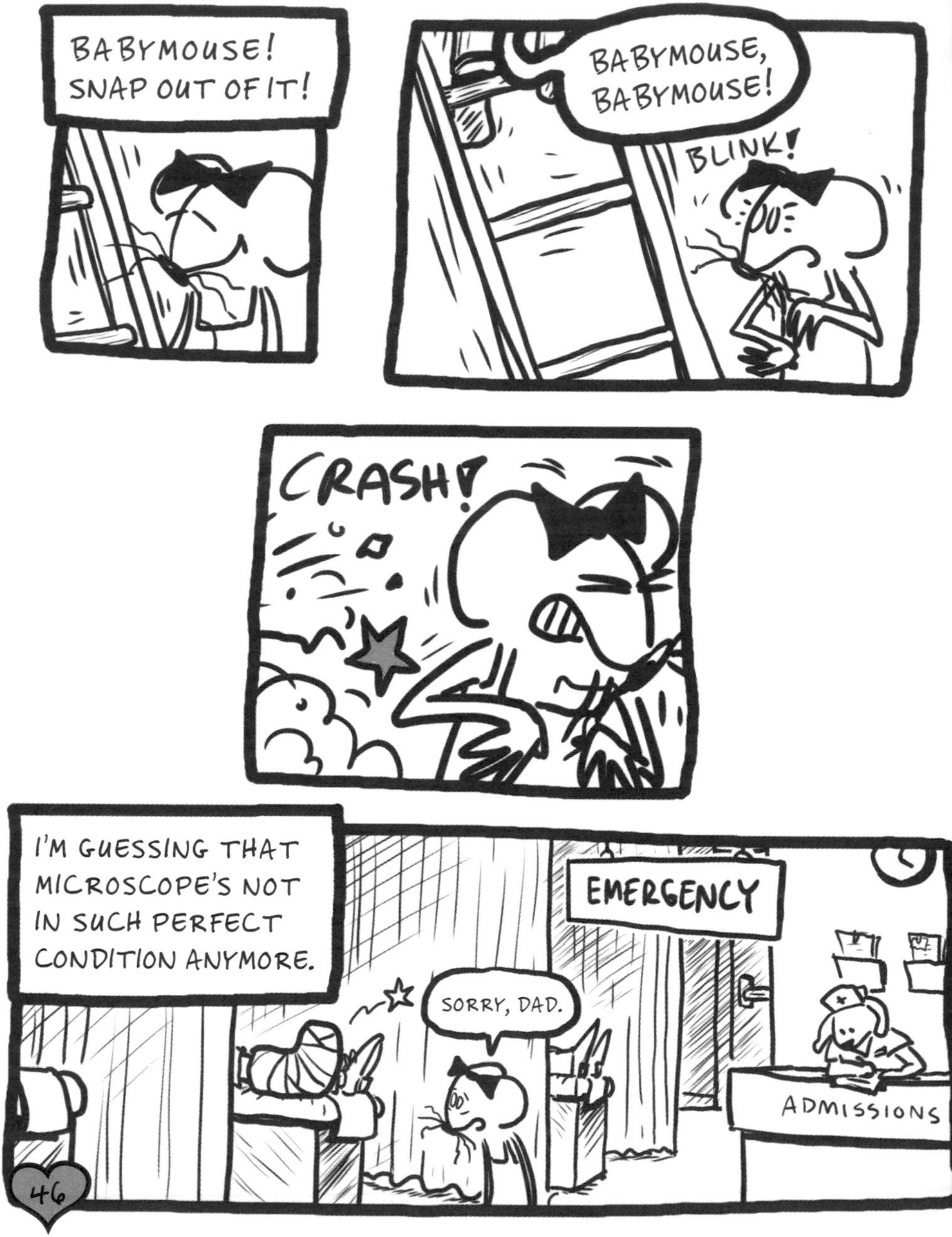
BABYMOUSE! SNAP OUT OF IT!
BABYMOUSE, BABYMOUSE!
BLINK!
CRASH!
I'M GUESSING THAT MICROSCOPE'S NOT IN SUCH PERFECT CONDITION ANYMORE.
EMERGENCY
SORRY, DAD.
ADMISSIONS

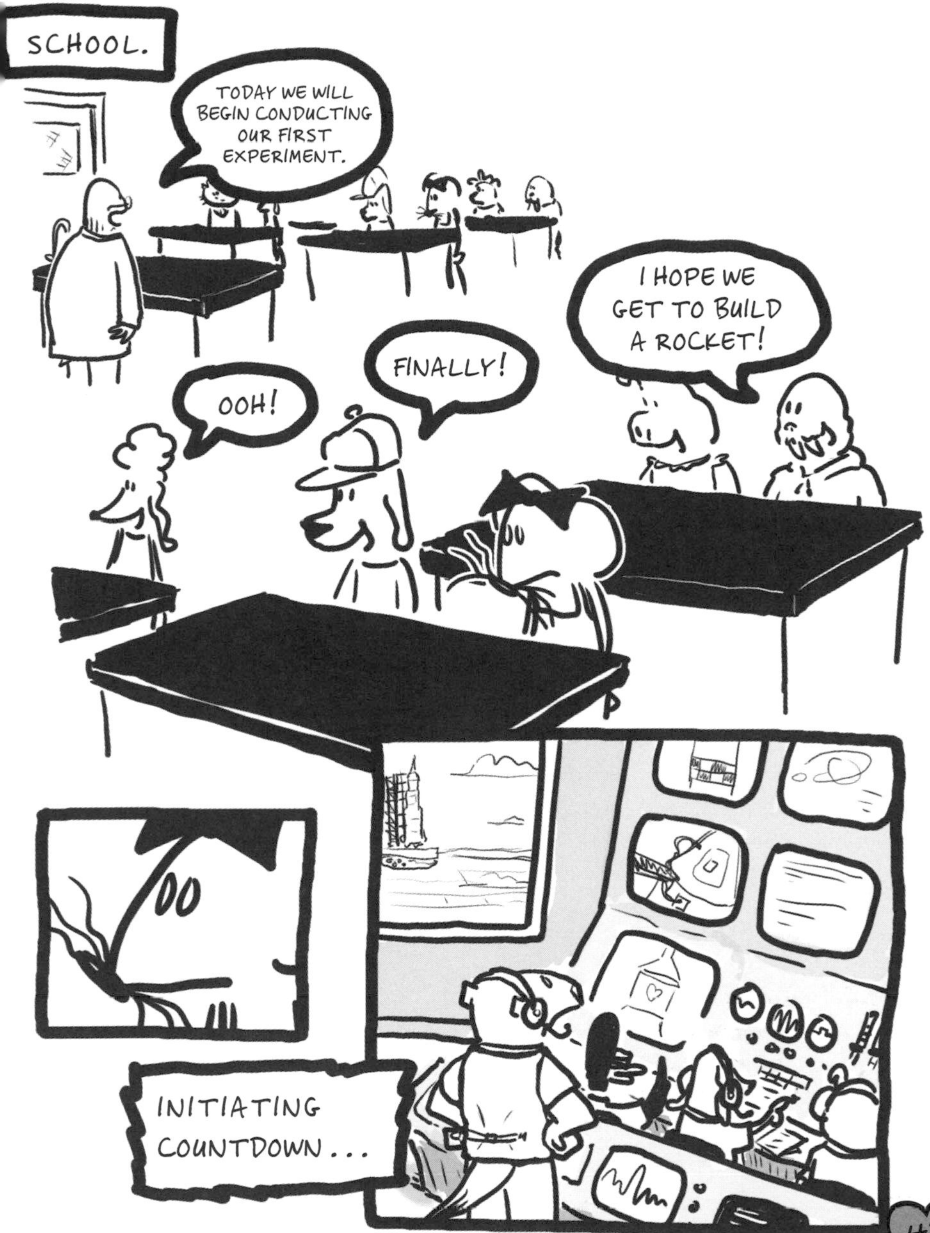
SCHOOL.
TODAY WE WILL BEGIN CONDUCTING OUR FIRST EXPERIMENT.
I HOPE WE GET TO BUILD A ROCKET!
FINALLY!
OOH!
INITIATING COUNTDOWN . . .

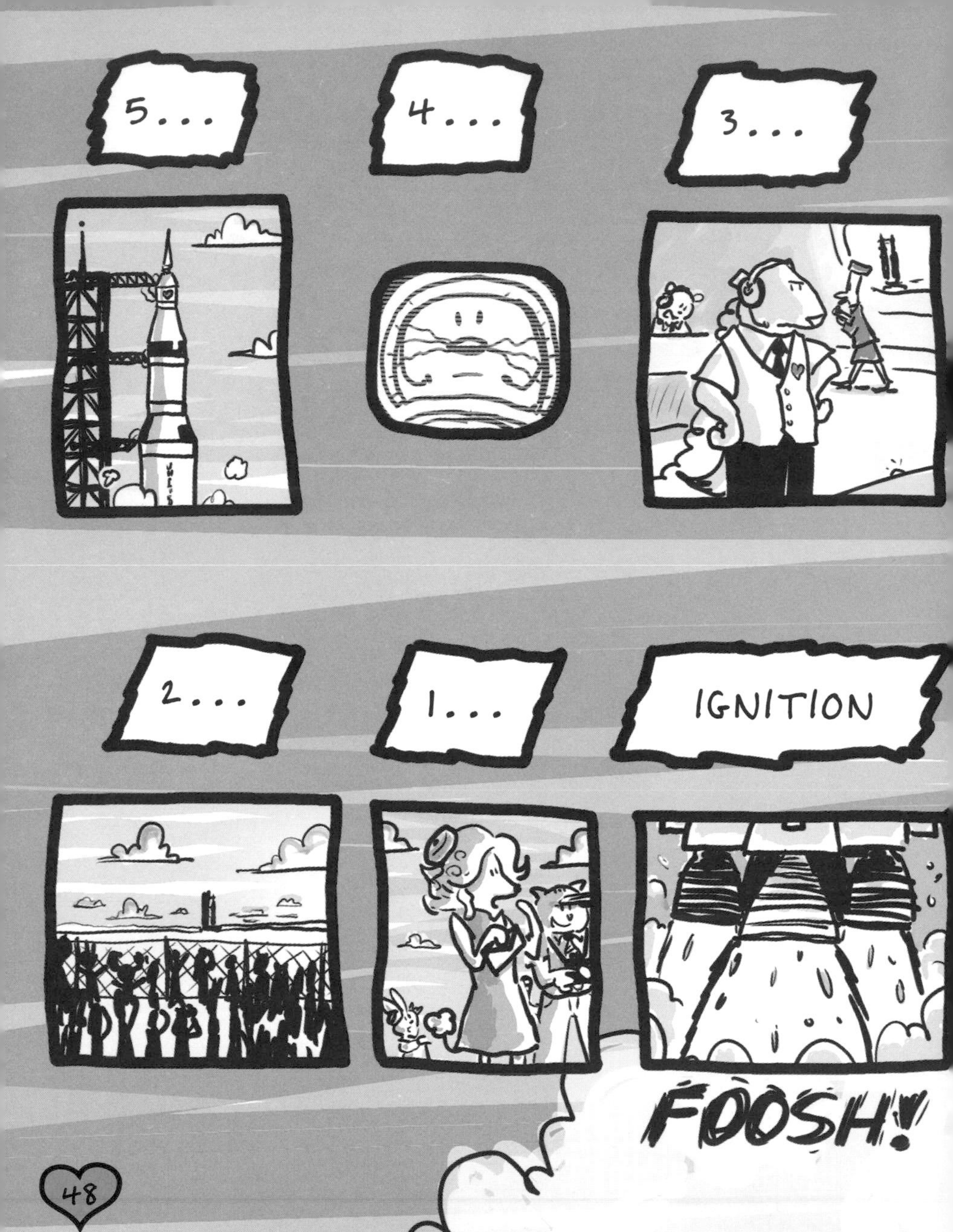
5...
4...
3...
2...
1...
IGNITION
FOOSH!

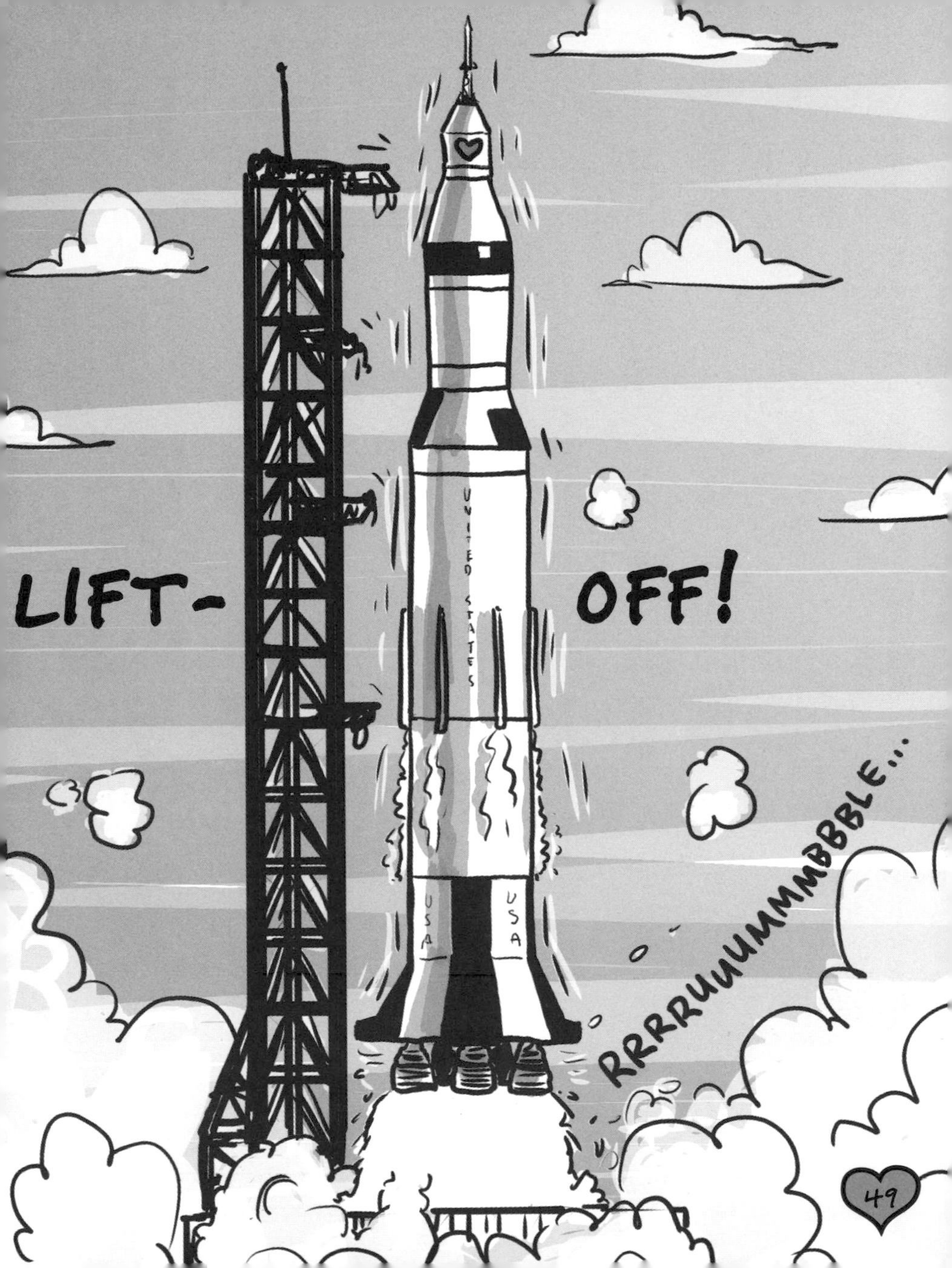
LIFT-
OFF!
UNITED STATES
USA
USA
RRRRUUUUMMMMBBBLE...

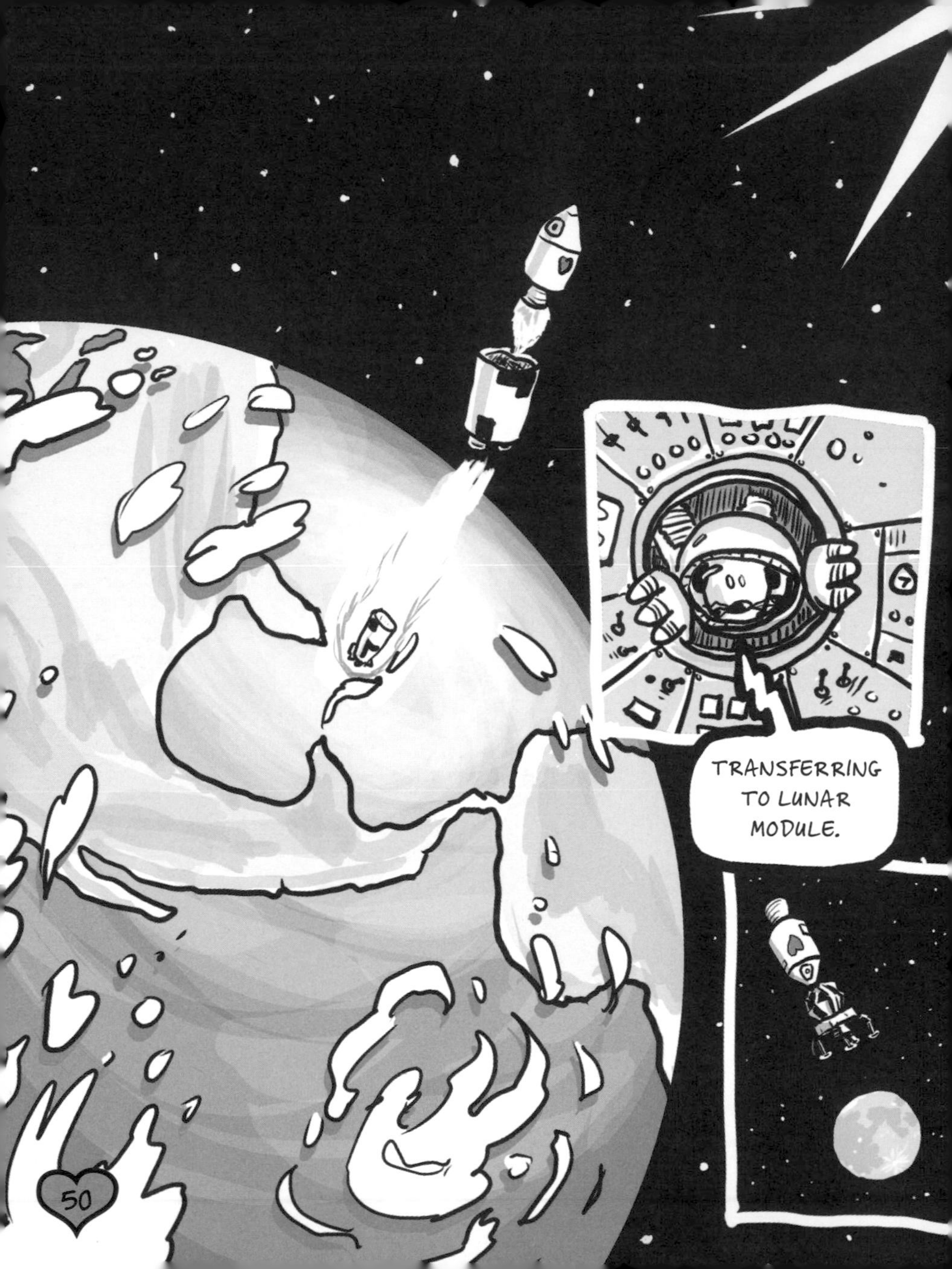
TRANSFERRING TO LUNAR MODULE.

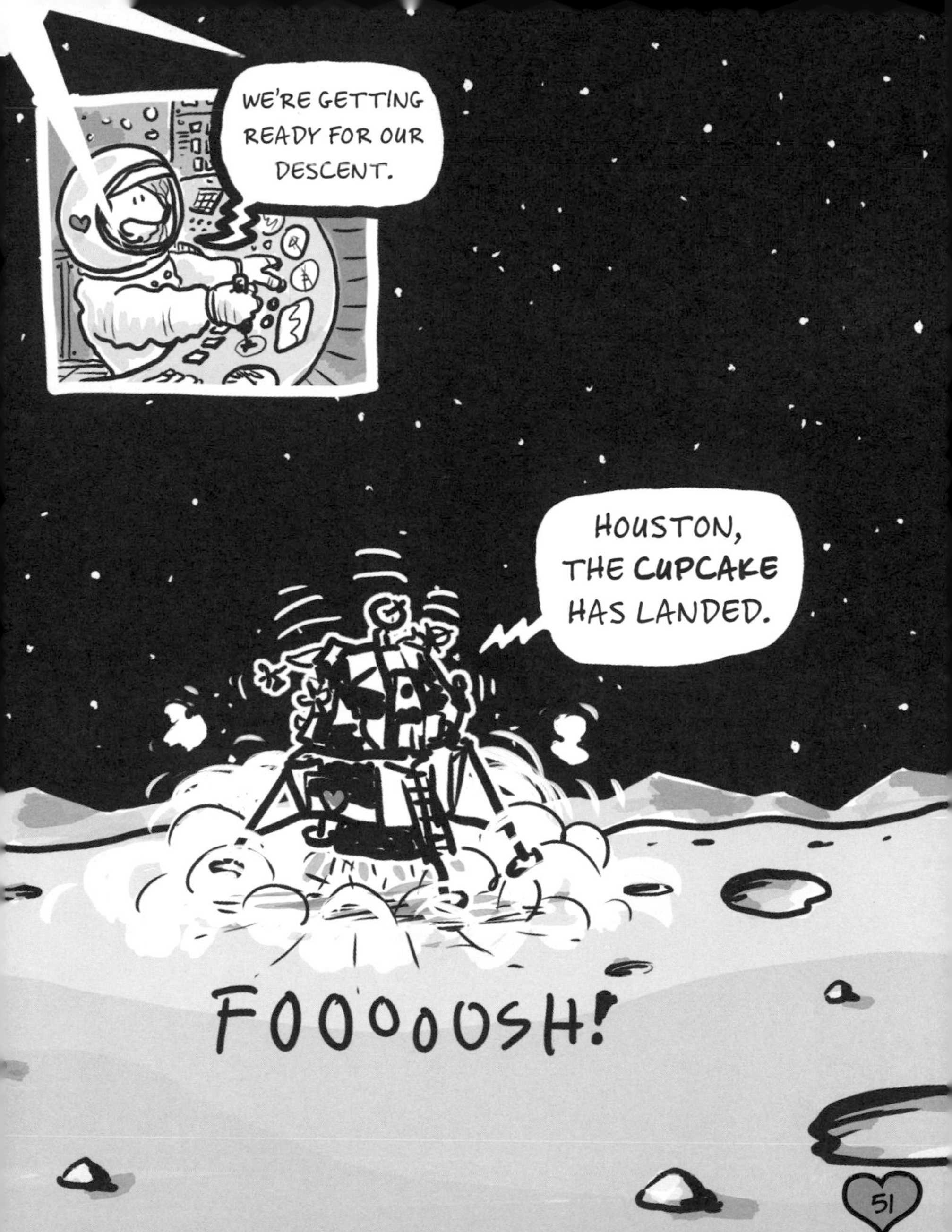

WE'RE GETTING READY FOR OUR DESCENT.
HOUSTON, THE **CUPCAKE** HAS LANDED.
FOOOOOSH!

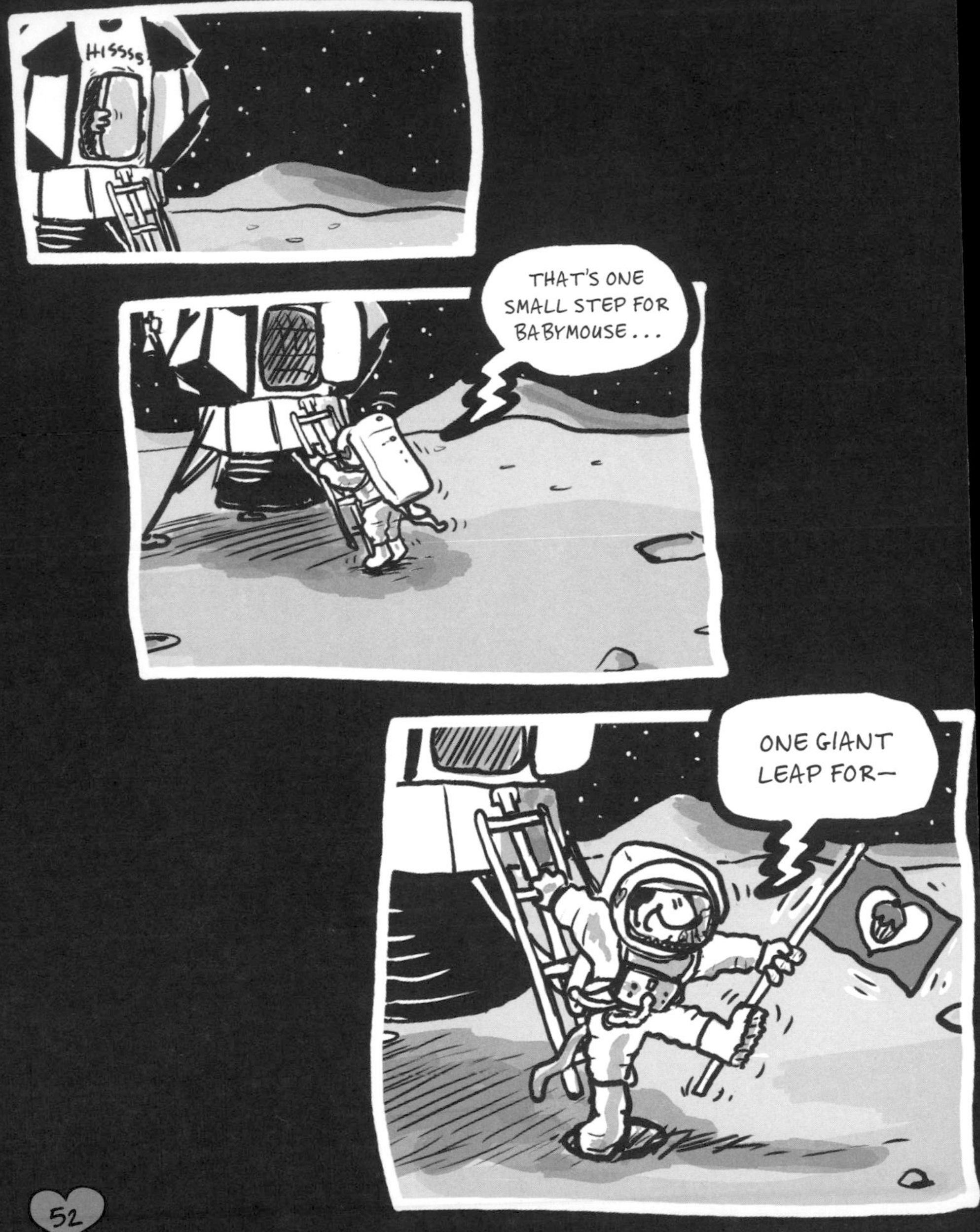
HISSSS
THAT'S ONE SMALL STEP FOR BABYMOUSE...
ONE GIANT LEAP FOR—

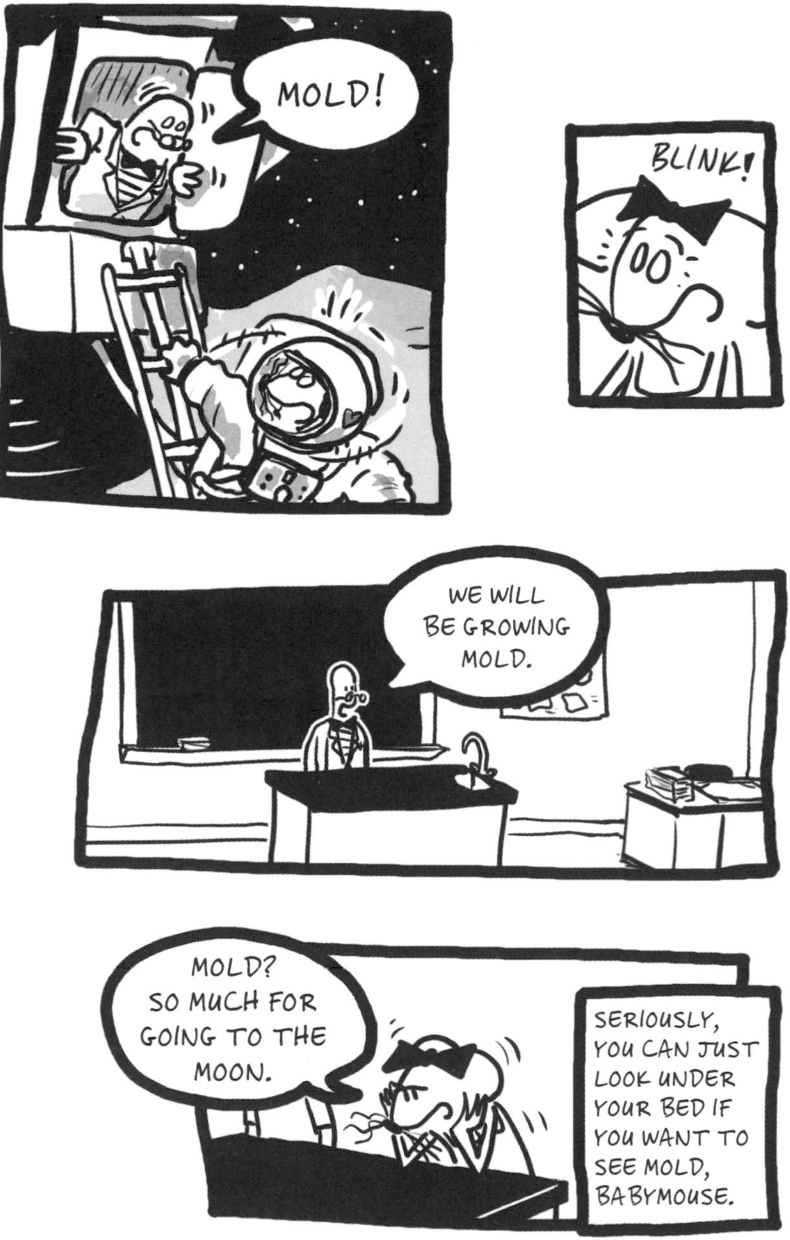
MOLD!
BLINK!
WE WILL BE GROWING MOLD.
MOLD? SO MUCH FOR GOING TO THE MOON.
SERIOUSLY, YOU CAN JUST LOOK UNDER YOUR BED IF YOU WANT TO SEE MOLD, BABYMOUSE.

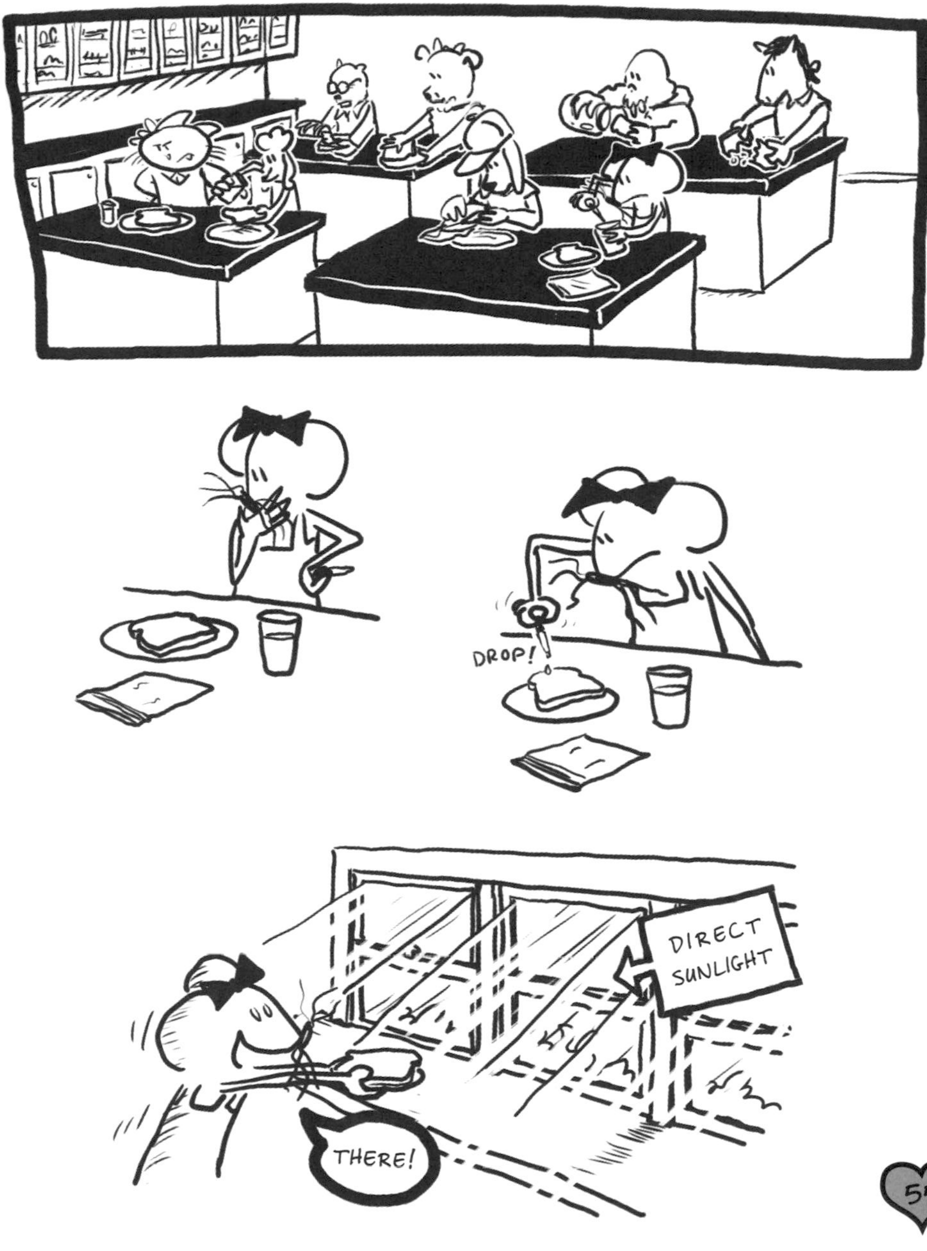
DROP!
DIRECT SUNLIGHT
THERE!

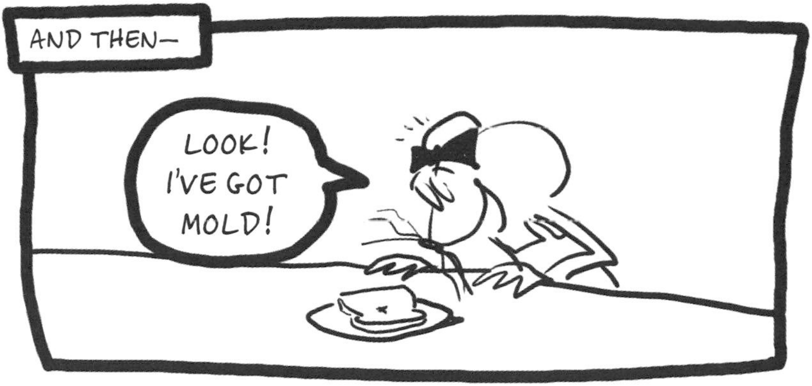
AND THEN—
LOOK! I'VE GOT MOLD!

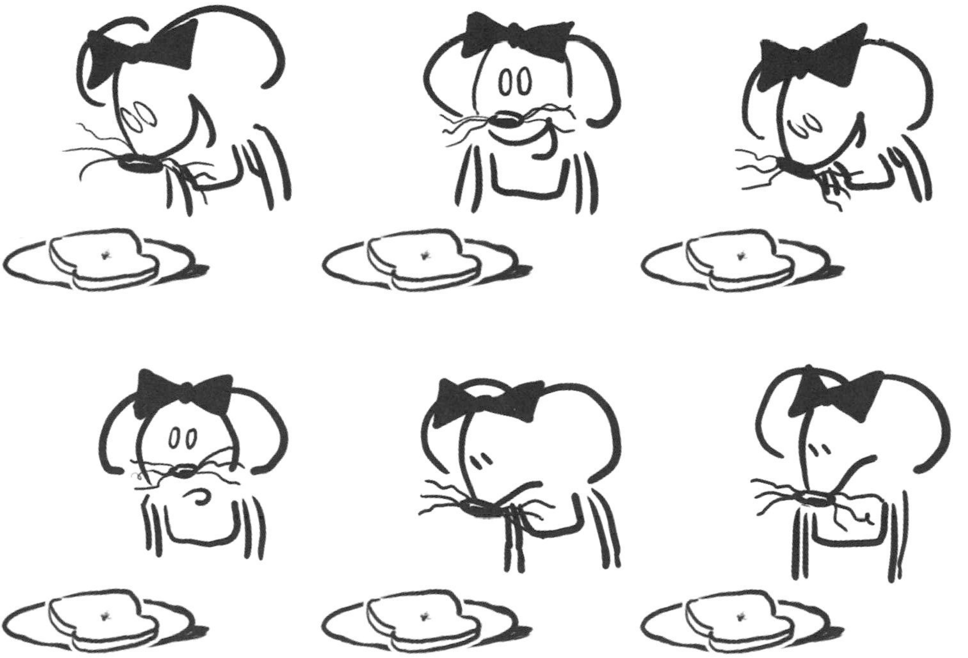

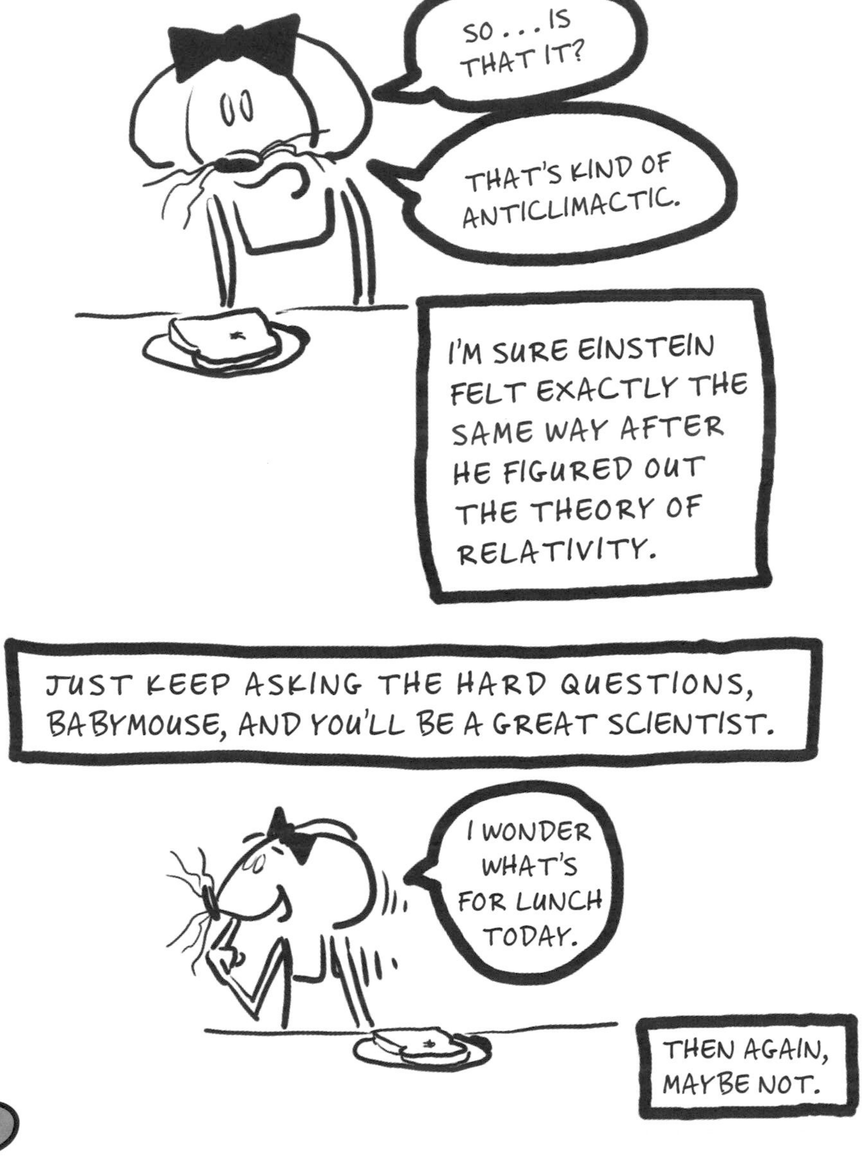
SO . . . IS THAT IT?
THAT'S KIND OF ANTICLIMACTIC.
I'M SURE EINSTEIN FELT EXACTLY THE SAME WAY AFTER HE FIGURED OUT THE THEORY OF RELATIVITY.
JUST KEEP ASKING THE HARD QUESTIONS, BABYMOUSE, AND YOU'LL BE A GREAT SCIENTIST.
I WONDER WHAT'S FOR LUNCH TODAY.
THEN AGAIN, MAYBE NOT.

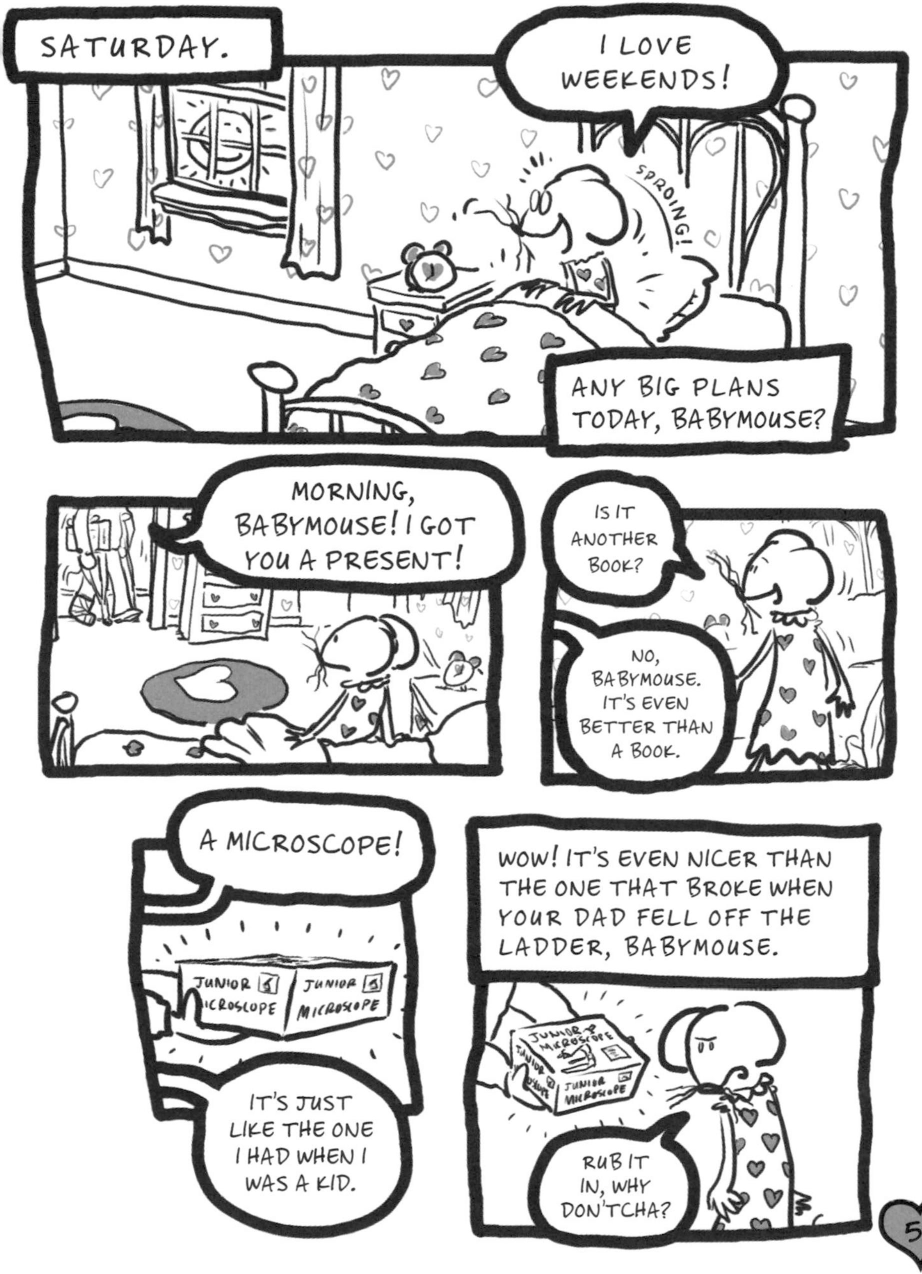
SATURDAY.
I LOVE WEEKENDS!
SPROING!
ANY BIG PLANS TODAY, BABYMOUSE?
MORNING, BABYMOUSE! I GOT YOU A PRESENT!
IS IT ANOTHER BOOK?
NO, BABYMOUSE. IT'S EVEN BETTER THAN A BOOK.
A MICROSCOPE!
JUNIOR MICROSCOPE
JUNIOR MICROSCOPE
IT'S JUST LIKE THE ONE I HAD WHEN I WAS A KID.
WOW! IT'S EVEN NICER THAN THE ONE THAT BROKE WHEN YOUR DAD FELL OFF THE LADDER, BABYMOUSE.
JUNIOR MICROSCOPE
RUB IT IN, WHY DON'TCHA?

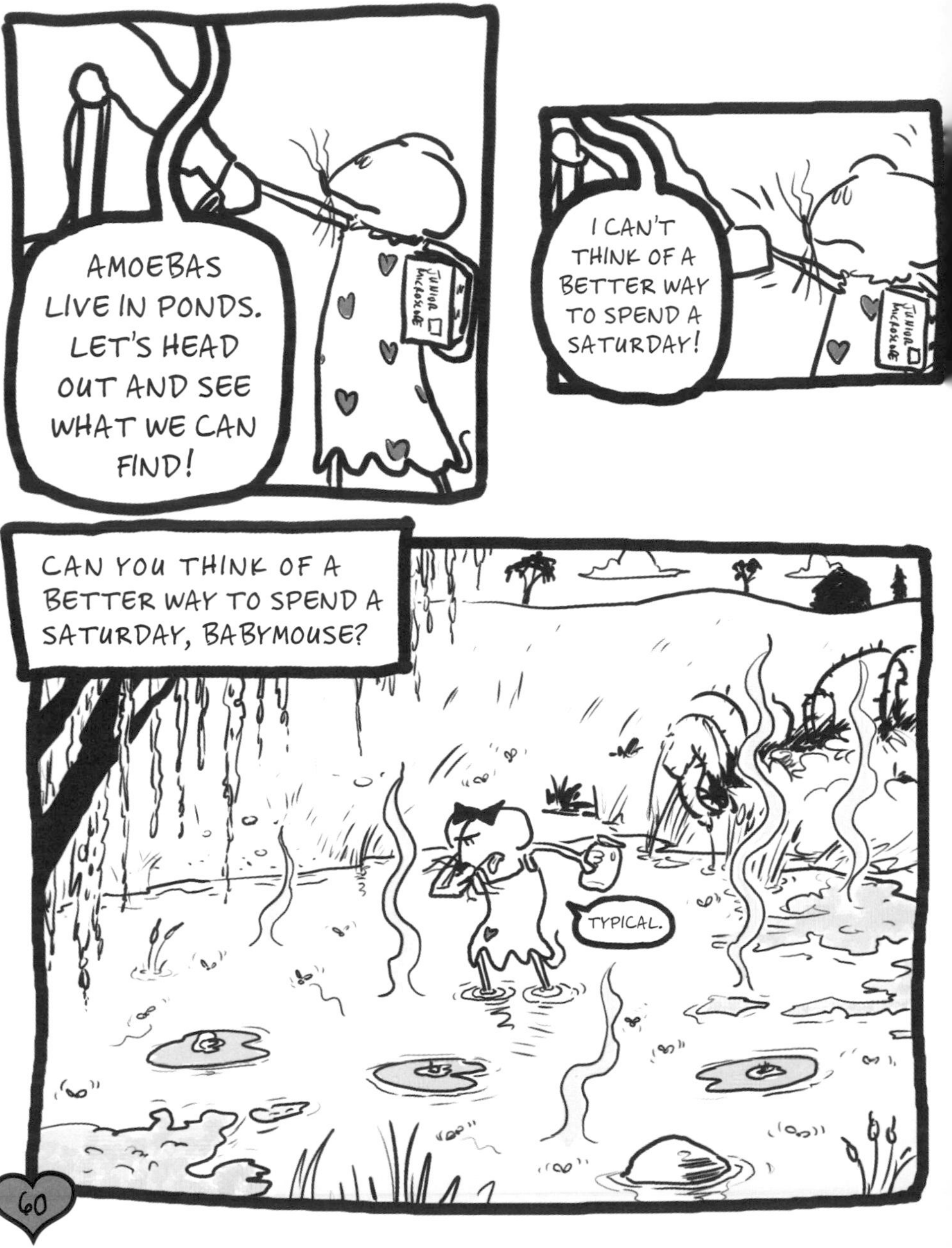
AMOEBAS LIVE IN PONDS. LET'S HEAD OUT AND SEE WHAT WE CAN FIND!
JUNIOR MICROSCOPE
I CAN'T THINK OF A BETTER WAY TO SPEND A SATURDAY!
JUNIOR MICROSCOPE
CAN YOU THINK OF A BETTER WAY TO SPEND A SATURDAY, BABYMOUSE?
TYPICAL.

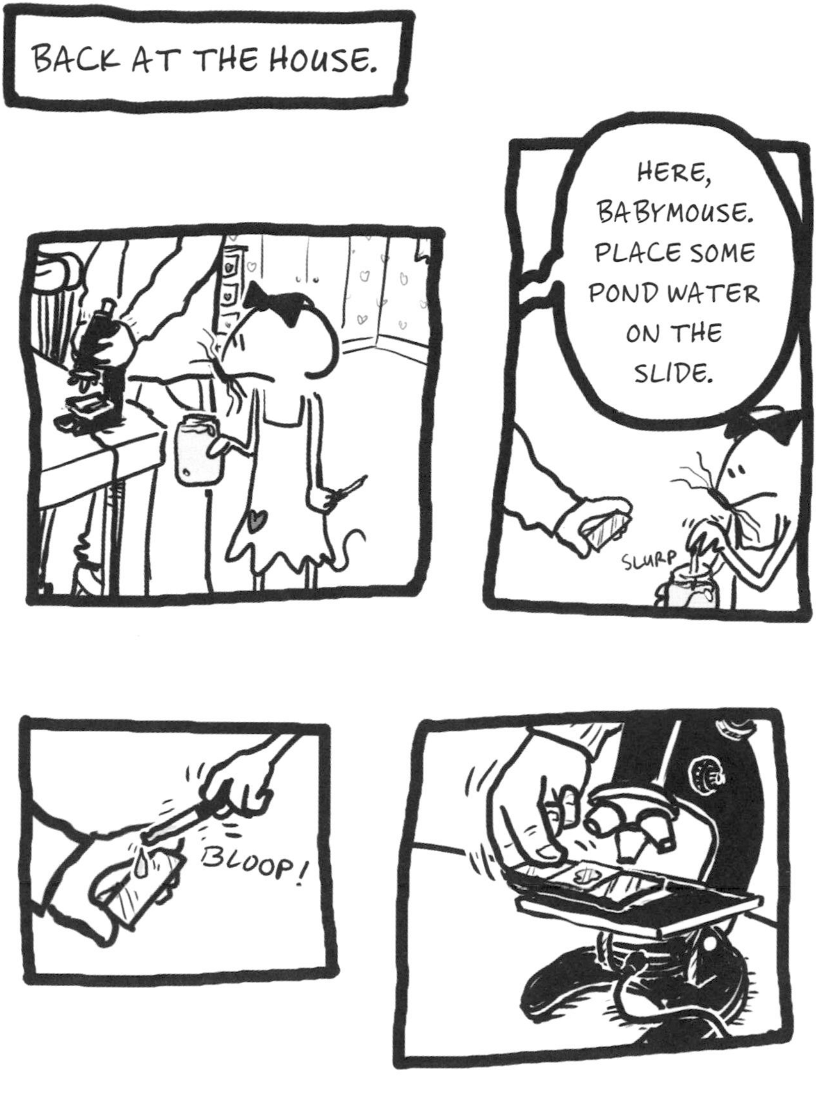
BACK AT THE HOUSE.
HERE, BABYMOUSE. PLACE SOME POND WATER ON THE SLIDE.
SLURP
BLOOP!

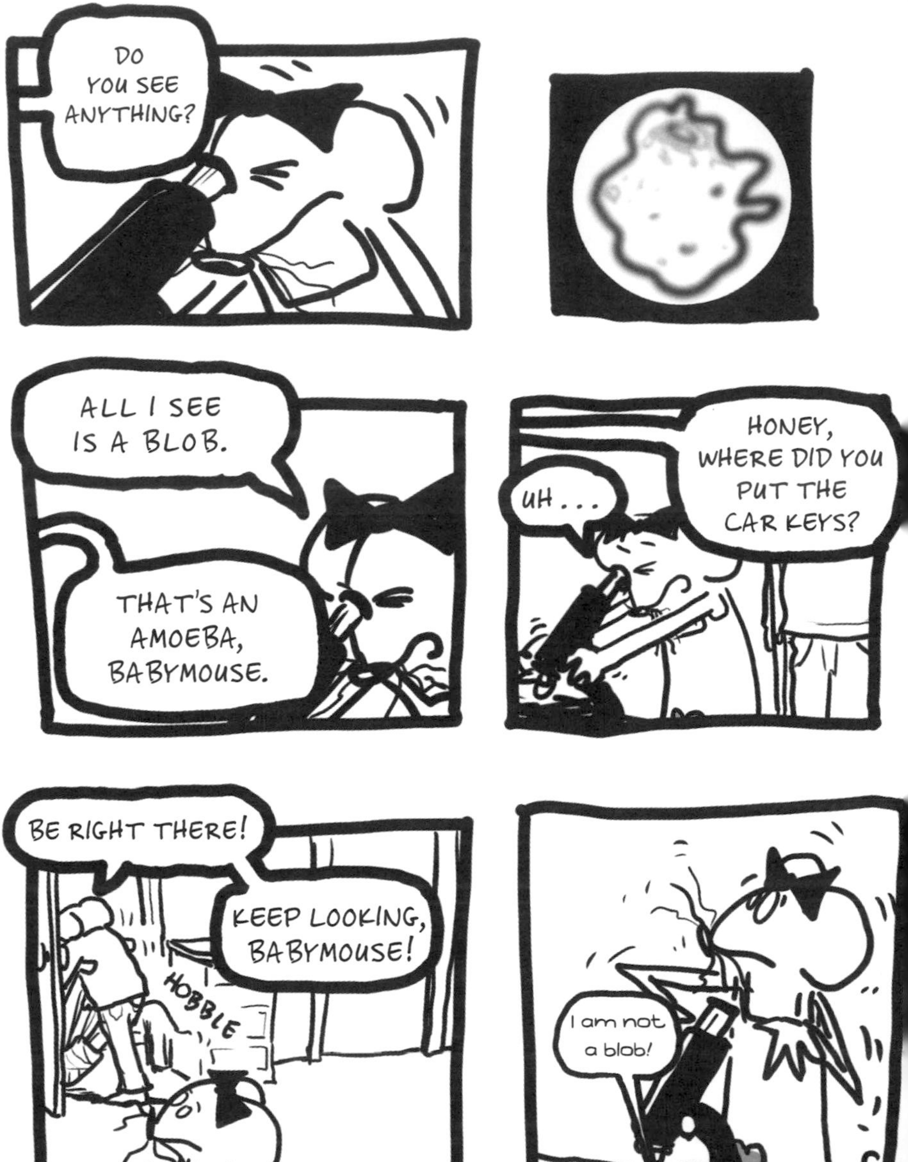
DO YOU SEE ANYTHING?
ALL I SEE IS A BLOB.
THAT'S AN AMOEBA, BABYMOUSE.
HONEY, WHERE DID YOU PUT THE CAR KEYS?
UH . . .
BE RIGHT THERE!
KEEP LOOKING, BABYMOUSE!
HOBBLE
I am not a blob!

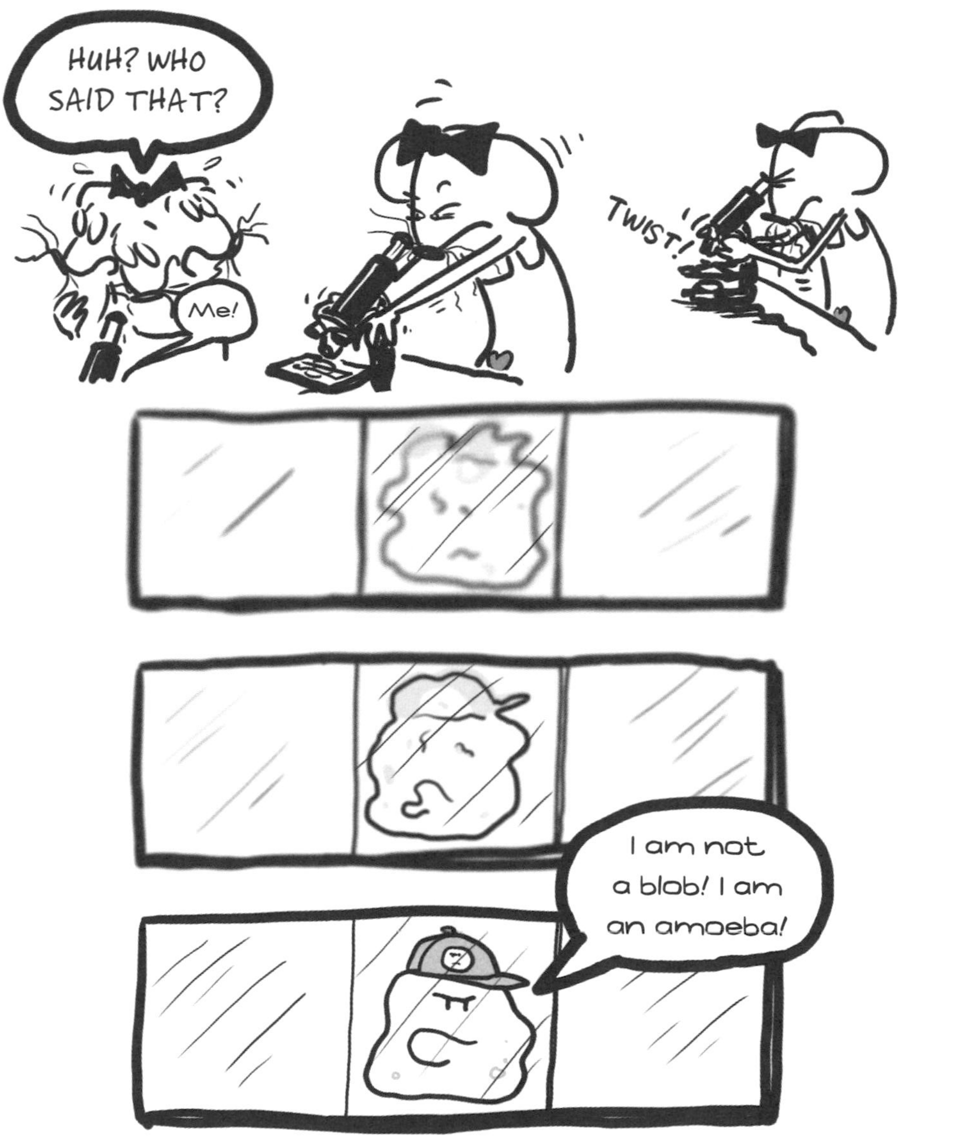
HUH? WHO SAID THAT?
Me!
TWIST!
I am not a blob! I am an amoeba!

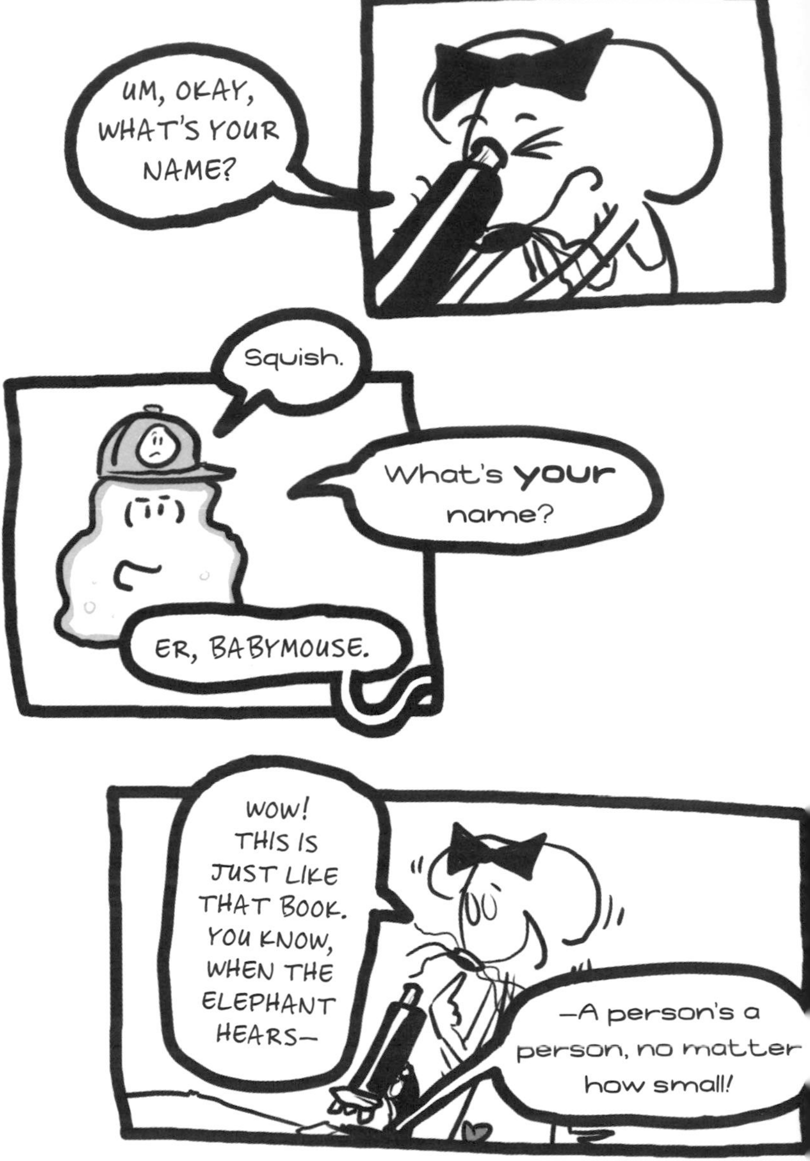
UM, OKAY, WHAT'S YOUR NAME?
Squish.
What's **your** name?
ER, BABYMOUSE.
WOW! THIS IS JUST LIKE THAT BOOK. YOU KNOW, WHEN THE ELEPHANT HEARS—
—A person's a person, no matter how small!

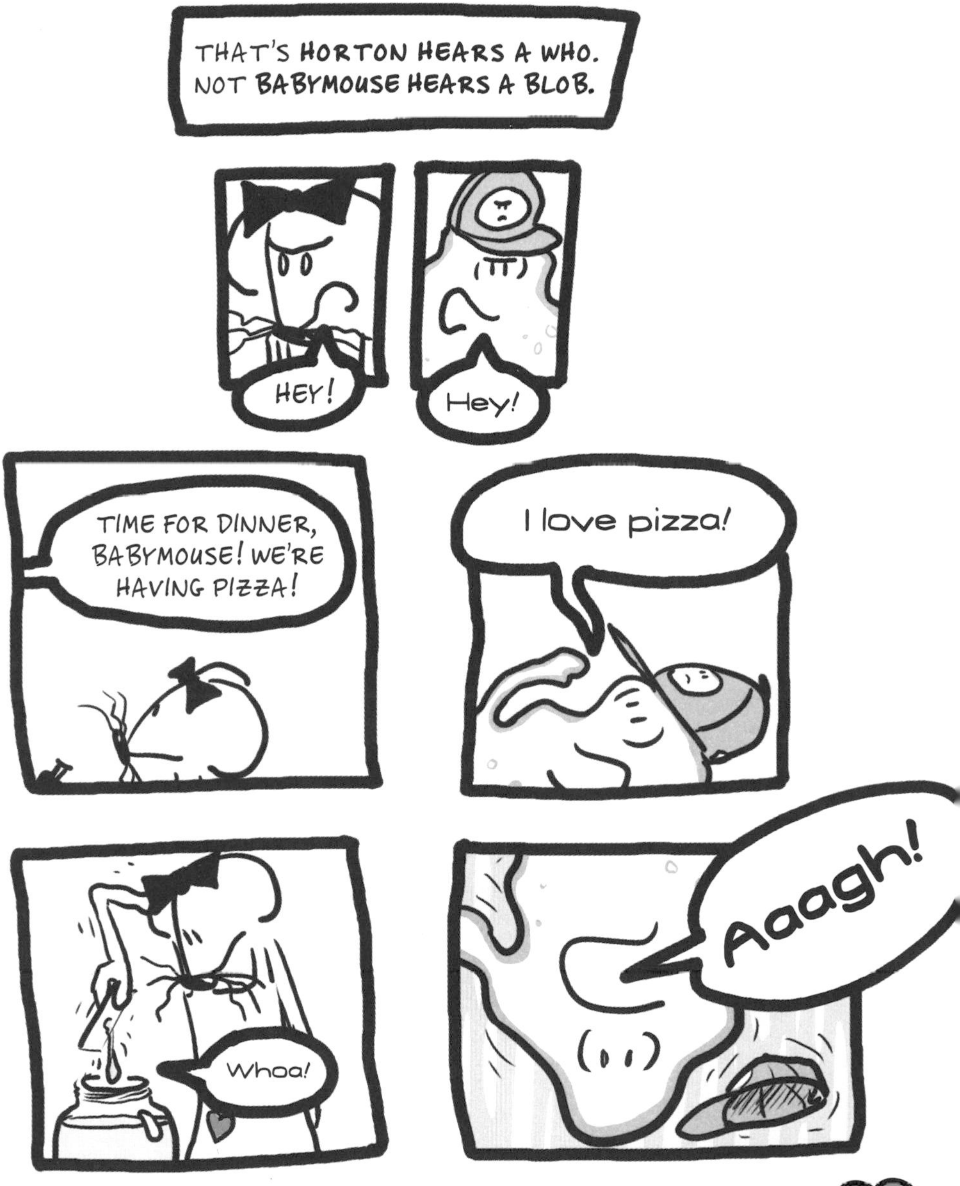
THAT'S **HORTON HEARS A WHO.**
NOT **BABYMOUSE HEARS A BLOB.**
HEY!
Hey!
TIME FOR DINNER, BABYMOUSE! WE'RE HAVING PIZZA!
I love pizza!
Whoa!
Aaagh!

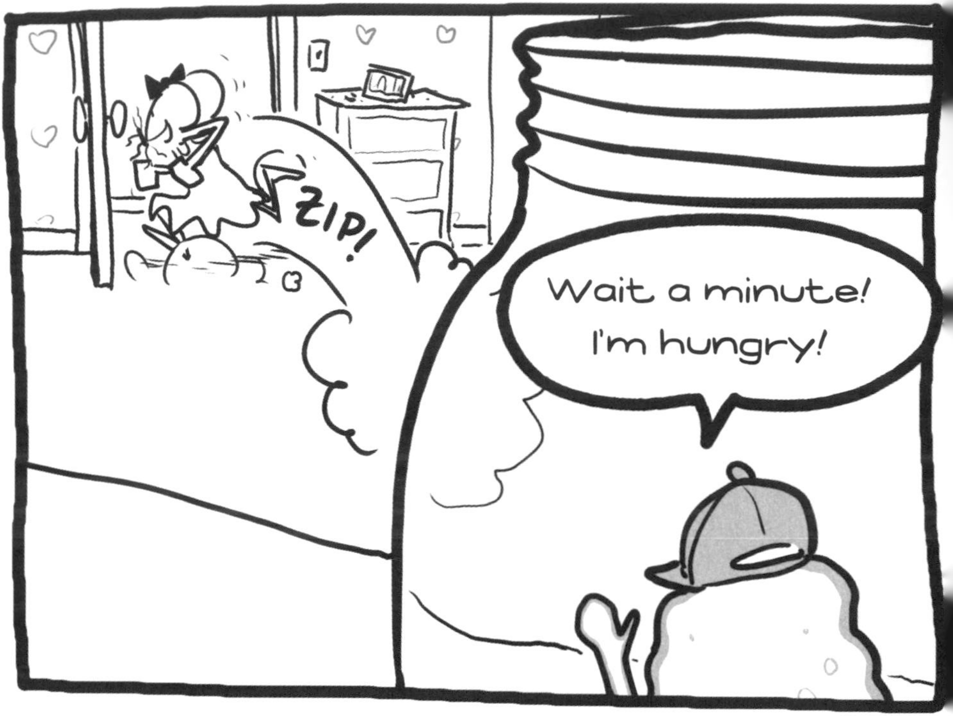
ZIP!
Wait a minute! I'm hungry!

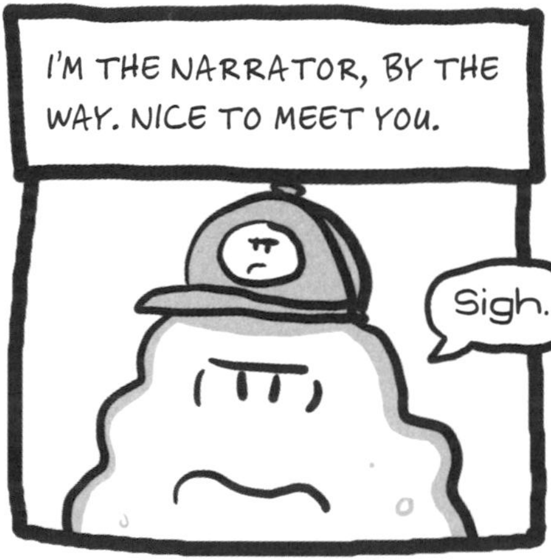
I'M THE NARRATOR, BY THE WAY. NICE TO MEET YOU.
Sigh.

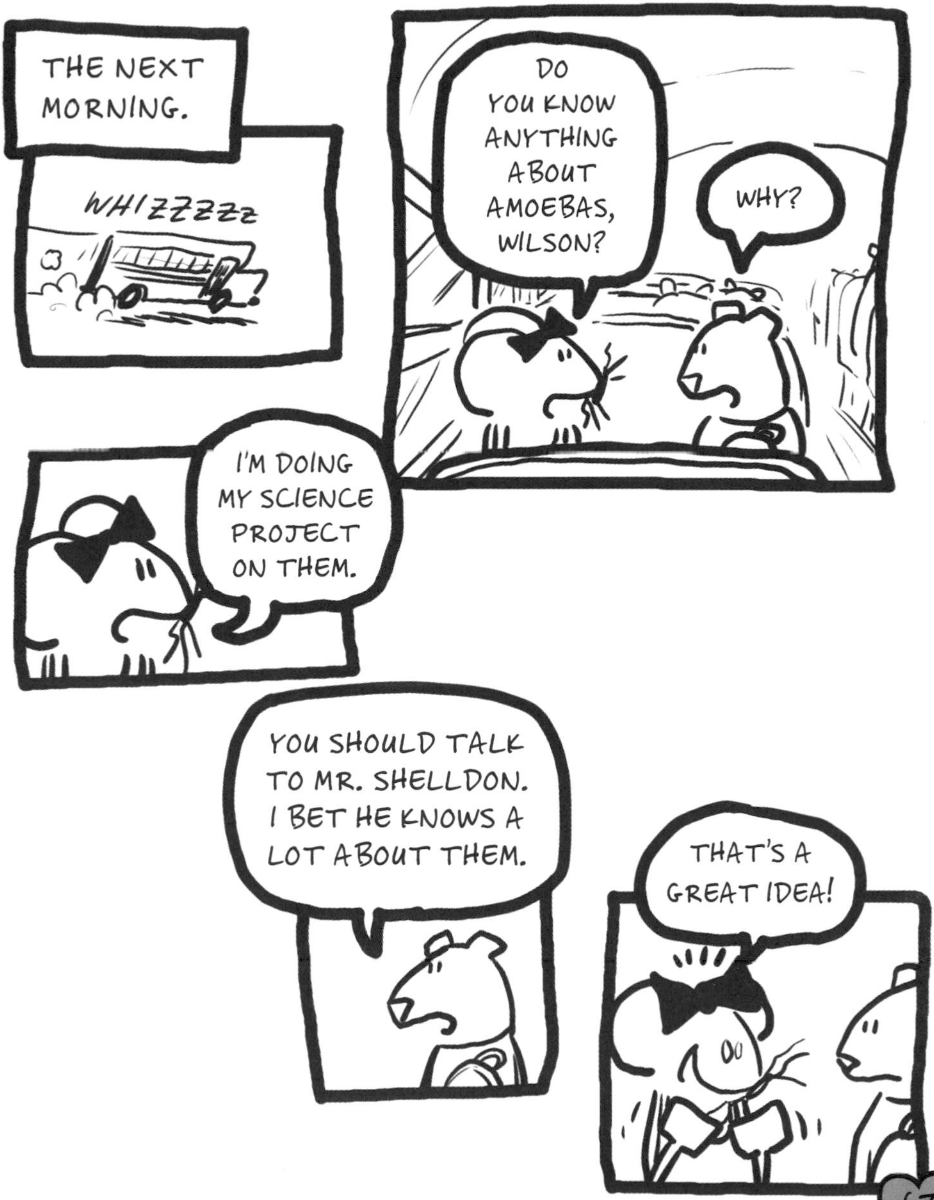
THE NEXT MORNING.
WHIZZZZZ
DO YOU KNOW ANYTHING ABOUT AMOEBAS, WILSON?
WHY?
I'M DOING MY SCIENCE PROJECT ON THEM.
YOU SHOULD TALK TO MR. SHELLDON. I BET HE KNOWS A LOT ABOUT THEM.
THAT'S A GREAT IDEA!

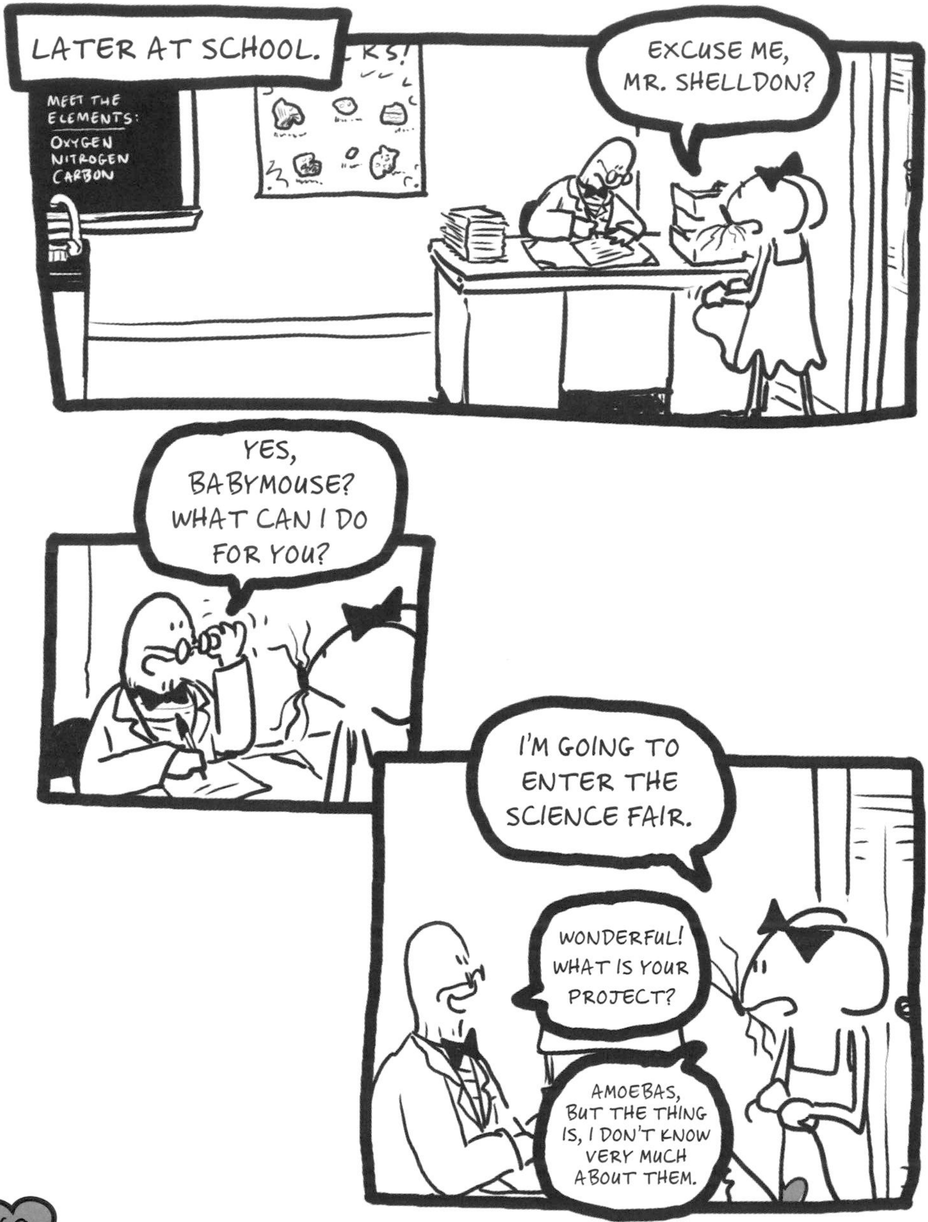
LATER AT SCHOOL.
MEET THE ELEMENTS:
OXYGEN
NITROGEN
CARBON
EXCUSE ME, MR. SHELLDON?
YES, BABYMOUSE? WHAT CAN I DO FOR YOU?
I'M GOING TO ENTER THE SCIENCE FAIR.
WONDERFUL! WHAT IS YOUR PROJECT?
AMOEBAS, BUT THE THING IS, I DON'T KNOW VERY MUCH ABOUT THEM.

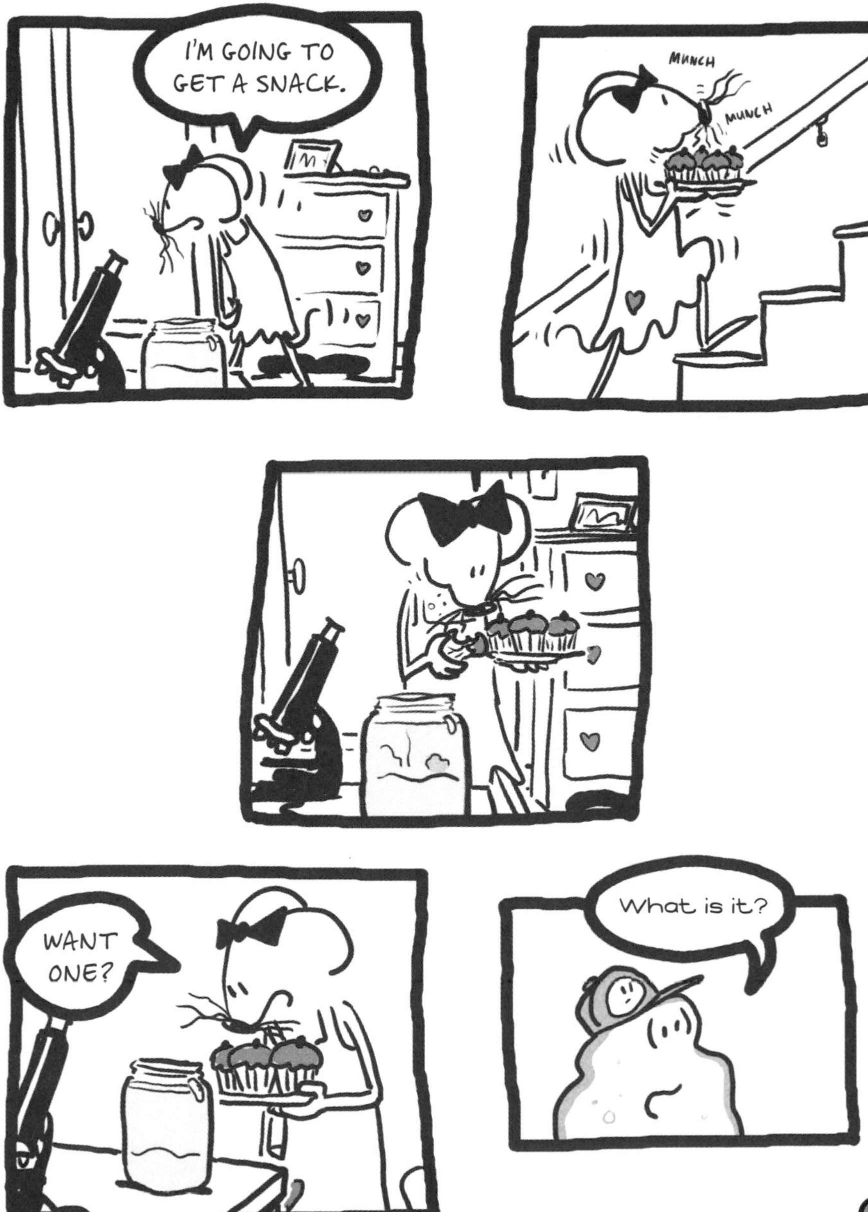
I'M GOING TO GET A SNACK.
MUNCH
MUNCH
WANT ONE?
What is it?

THE DAY OF THE SCIENCE FAIR.

COOL.

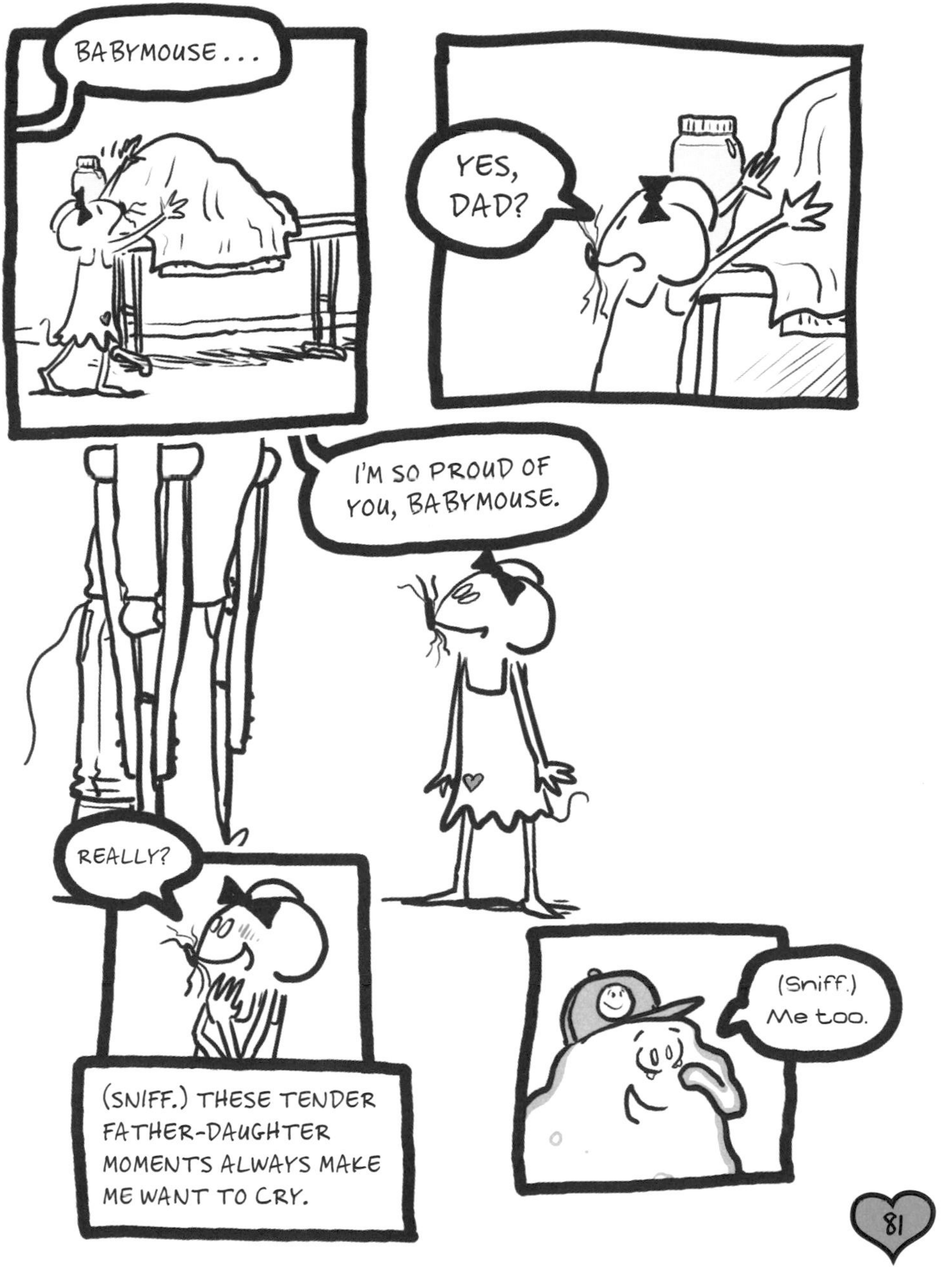
BABYMOUSE . . .
YES, DAD?
I'M SO PROUD OF YOU, BABYMOUSE.
REALLY?
(SNIFF.) THESE TENDER FATHER-DAUGHTER MOMENTS ALWAYS MAKE ME WANT TO CRY.
(Sniff.) Me too.

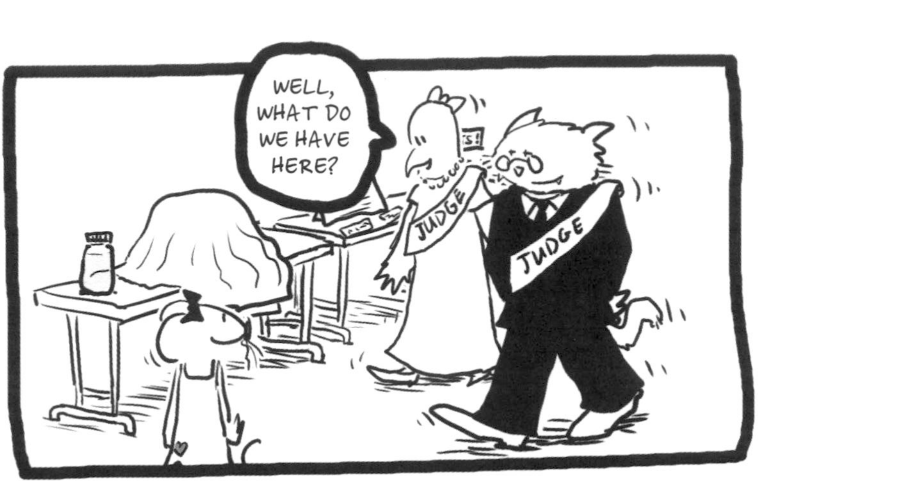
WELL, WHAT DO WE HAVE HERE?
JUDGE
JUDGE

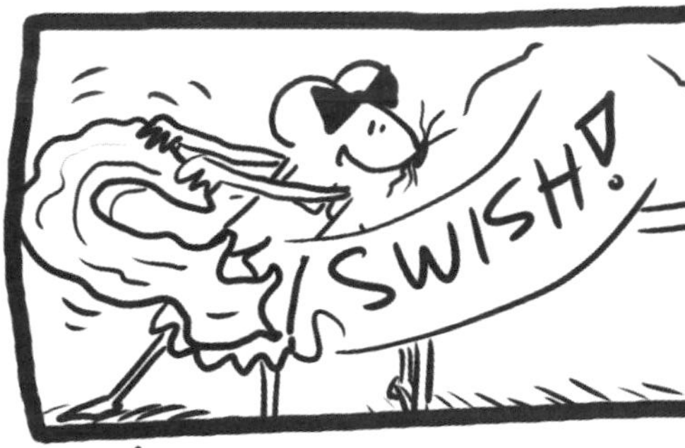
SWISH!

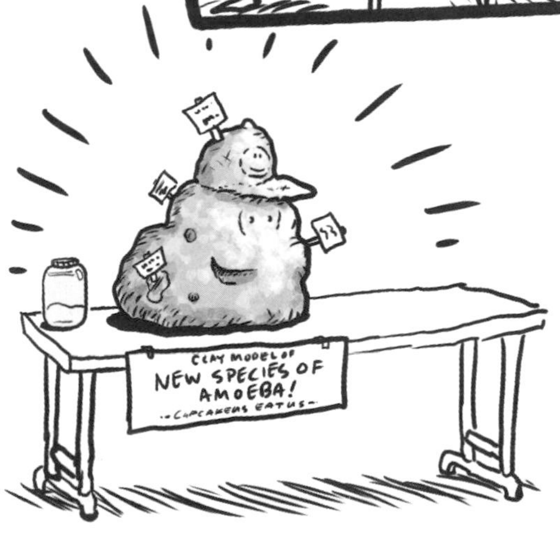
CLAY MODEL OF
NEW SPECIES OF AMOEBA!
CUPCAKEUS EATUS

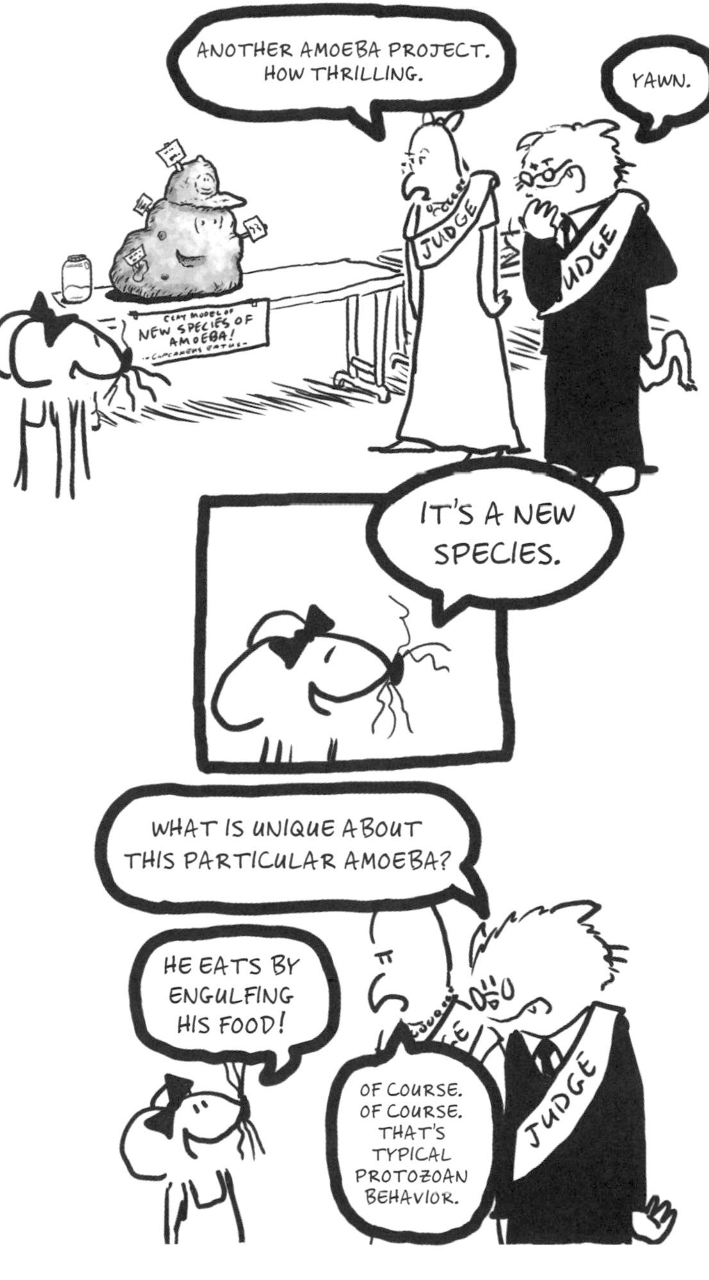
ANOTHER AMOEBA PROJECT. HOW THRILLING.
YAWN.
NEW SPECIES OF AMOEBA!
JUDGE
JUDGE
IT'S A NEW SPECIES.
WHAT IS UNIQUE ABOUT THIS PARTICULAR AMOEBA?
HE EATS BY ENGULFING HIS FOOD!
OF COURSE. OF COURSE. THAT'S TYPICAL PROTOZOAN BEHAVIOR.
JUDGE

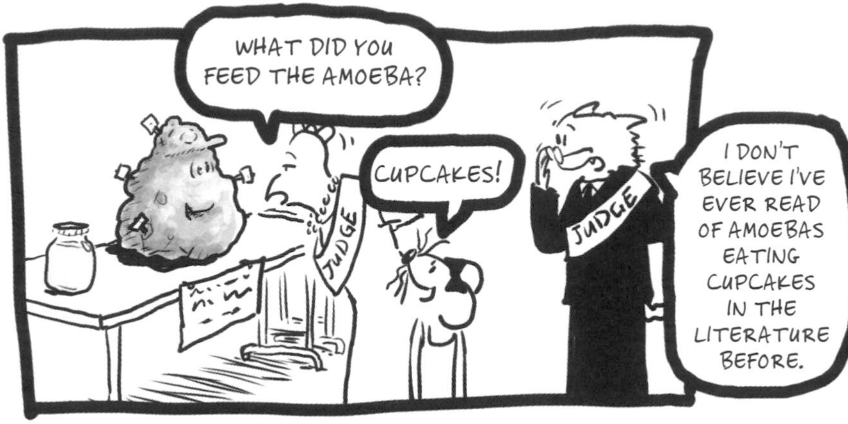
WHAT DID YOU FEED THE AMOEBA?
JUDGE
CUPCAKES!
JUDGE
I DON'T BELIEVE I'VE EVER READ OF AMOEBAS EATING CUPCAKES IN THE LITERATURE BEFORE.

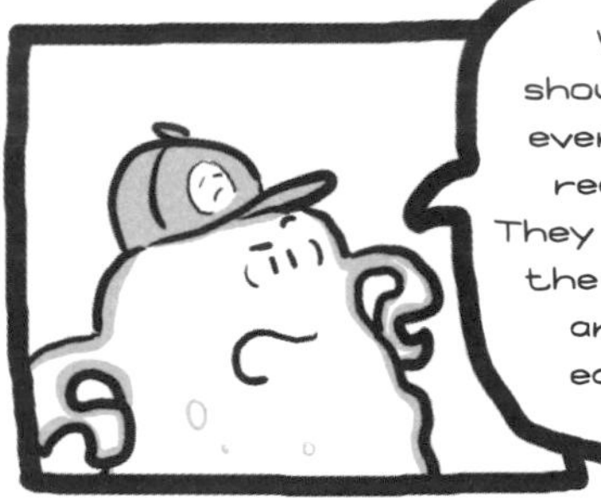
Well, you shouldn't believe everything you read in books. They used to think the sun orbited around the earth, too!

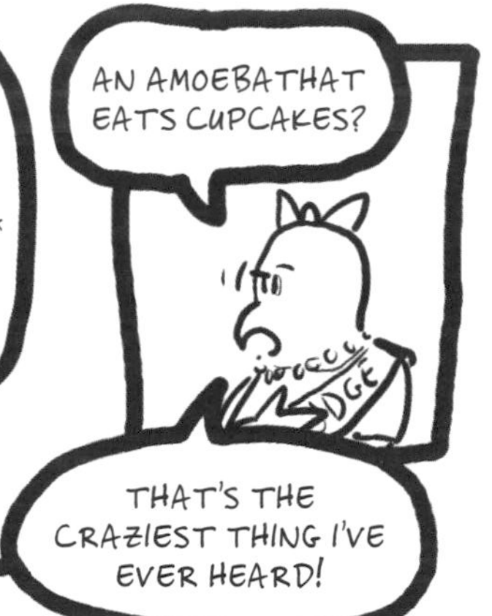
AN AMOEBATHAT EATS CUPCAKES?
THAT'S THE CRAZIEST THING I'VE EVER HEARD!

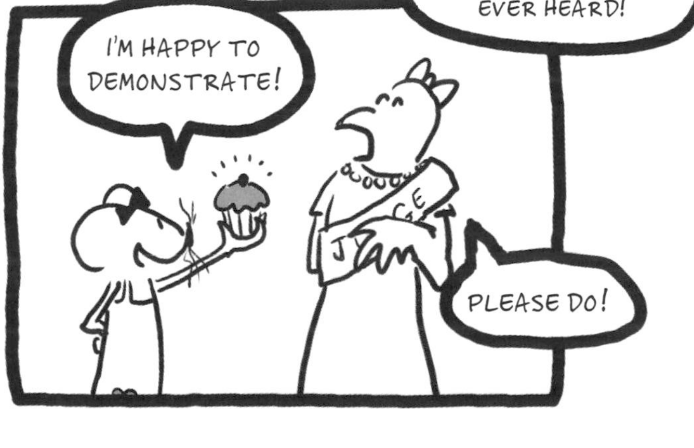
I'M HAPPY TO DEMONSTRATE!
PLEASE DO!

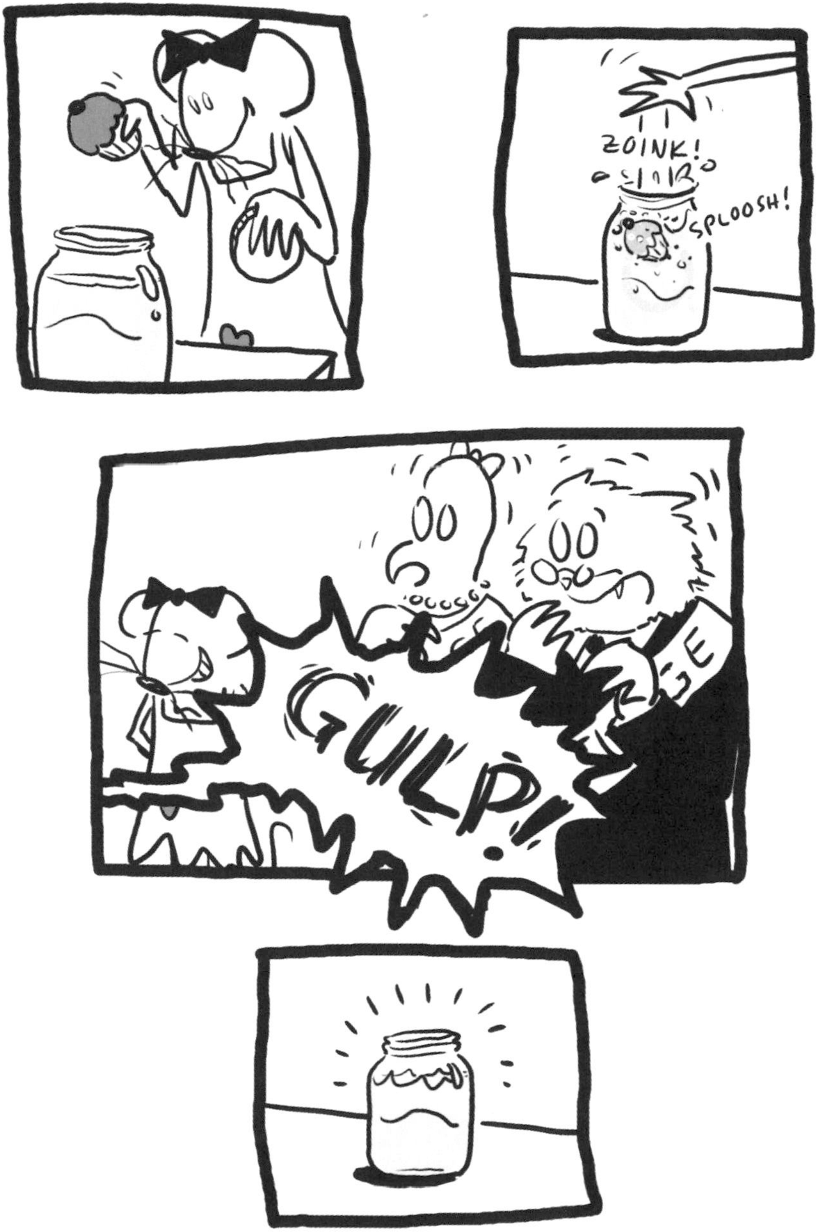
ZOINK!
SPLOOSH!
GULP!

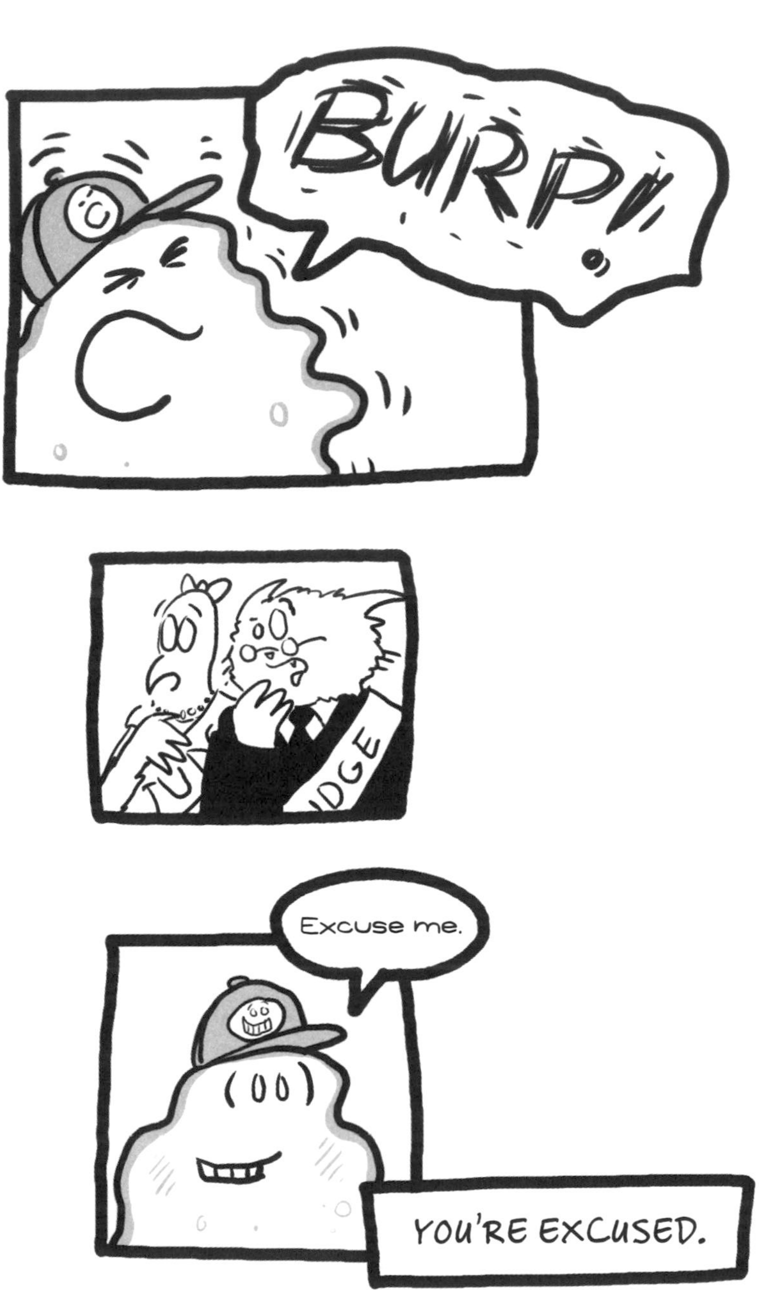
BURP!
Excuse me.
YOU'RE EXCUSED.

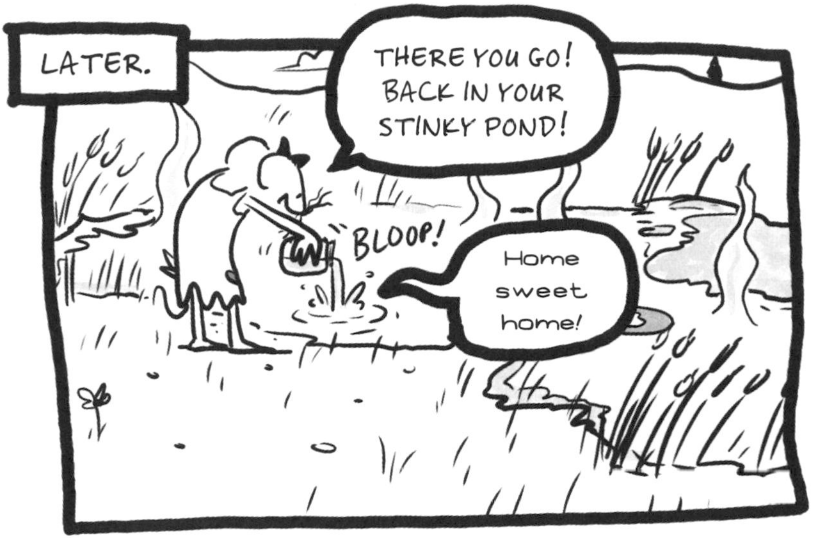
LATER.
THERE YOU GO! BACK IN YOUR STINKY POND!
BLOOP!
Home sweet home!

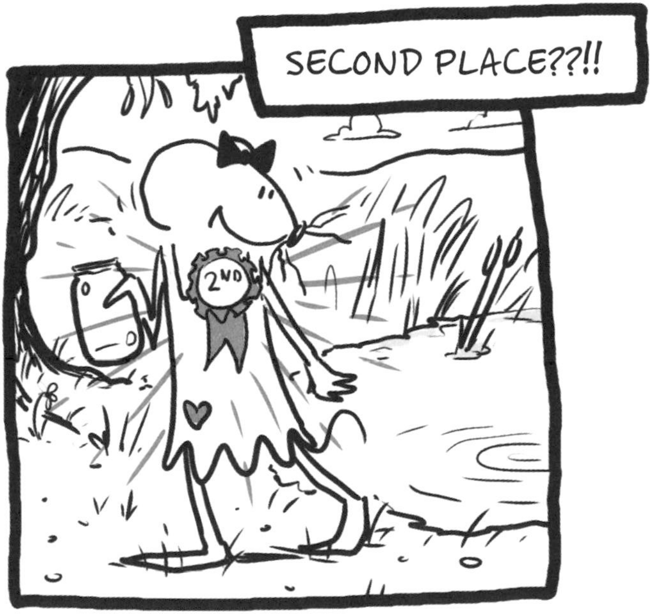
SECOND PLACE??!!
2ND

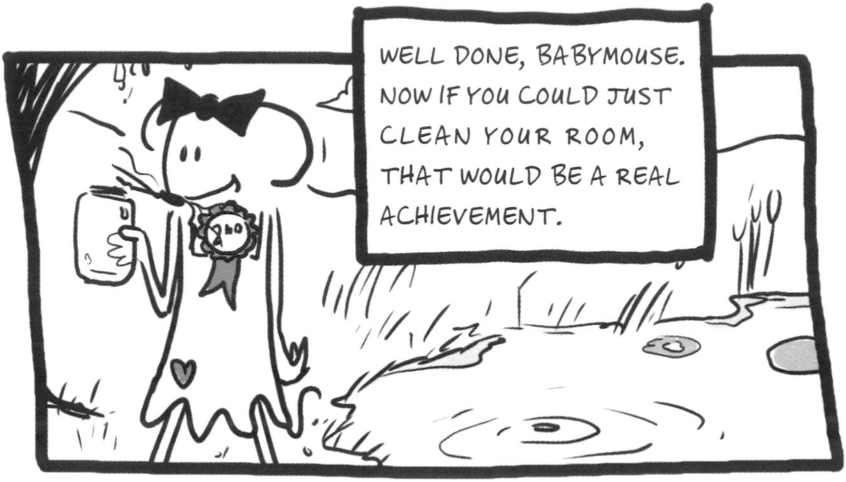
WELL DONE, BABYMOUSE. NOW IF YOU COULD JUST CLEAN YOUR ROOM, THAT WOULD BE A REAL ACHIEVEMENT.

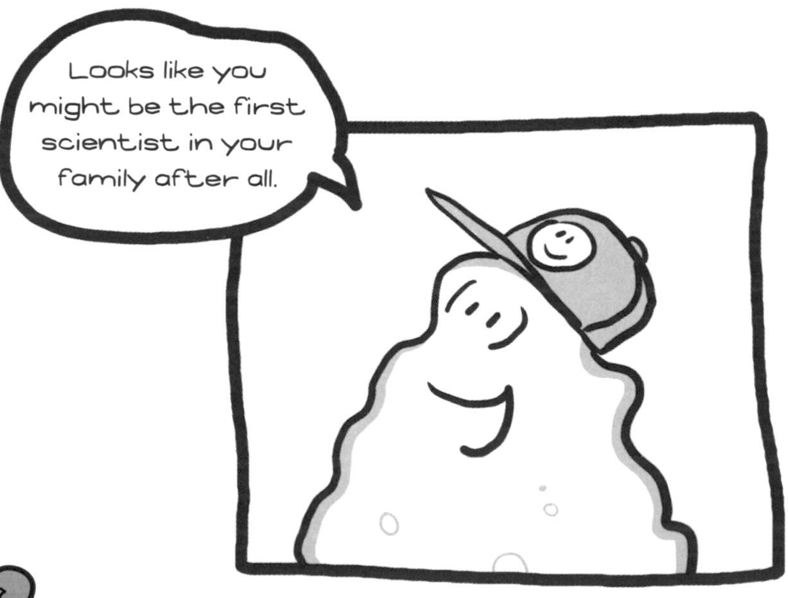
Looks like you might be the first scientist in your family after all.

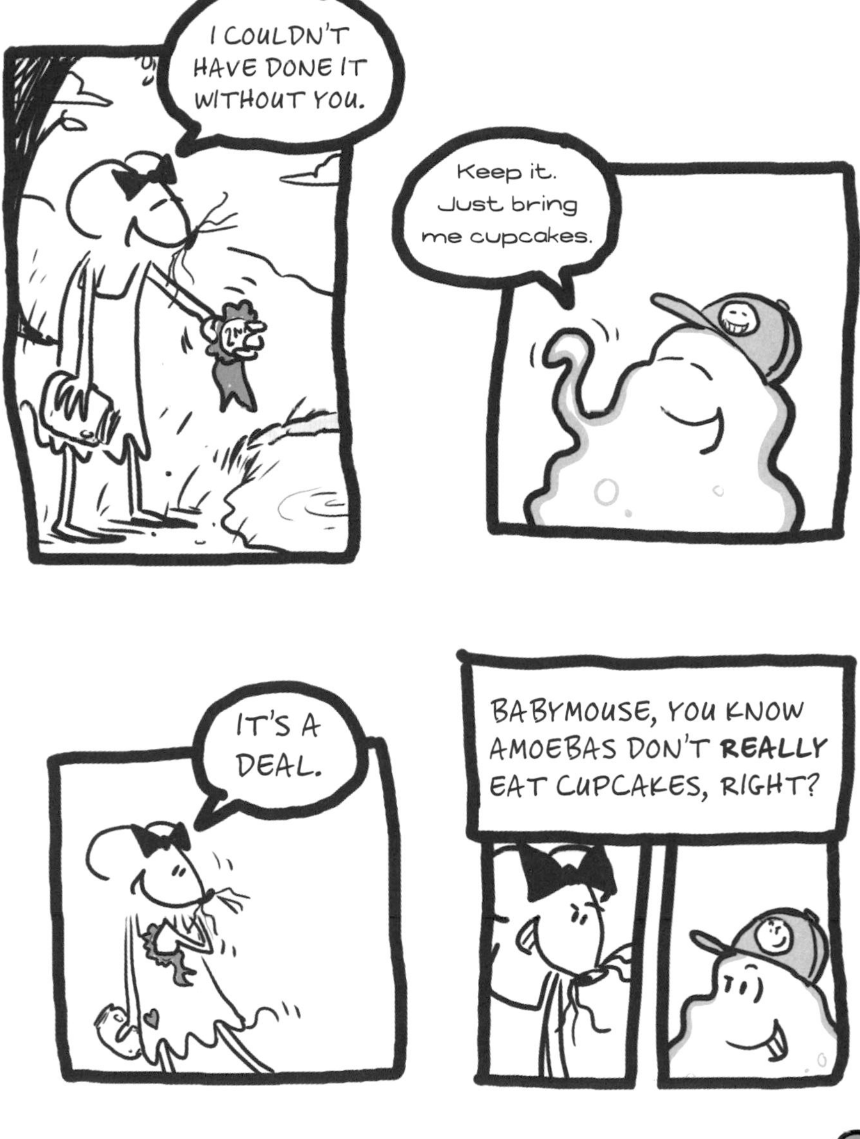
I COULDN'T HAVE DONE IT WITHOUT YOU.
2ND
Keep it. Just bring me cupcakes.
IT'S A DEAL.
BABYMOUSE, YOU KNOW AMOEBAS DON'T **REALLY** EAT CUPCAKES, RIGHT?

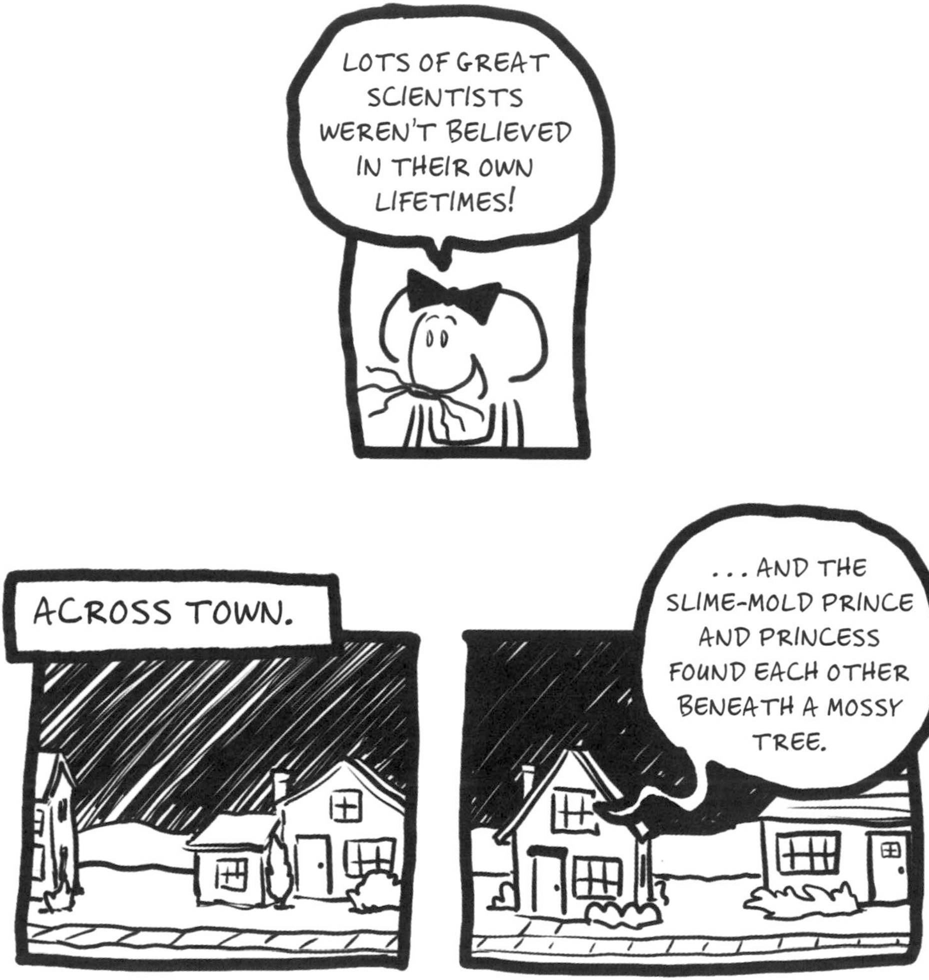
LOTS OF GREAT SCIENTISTS WEREN'T BELIEVED IN THEIR OWN LIFETIMES!
ACROSS TOWN.
. . . AND THE SLIME-MOLD PRINCE AND PRINCESS FOUND EACH OTHER BENEATH A MOSSY TREE.

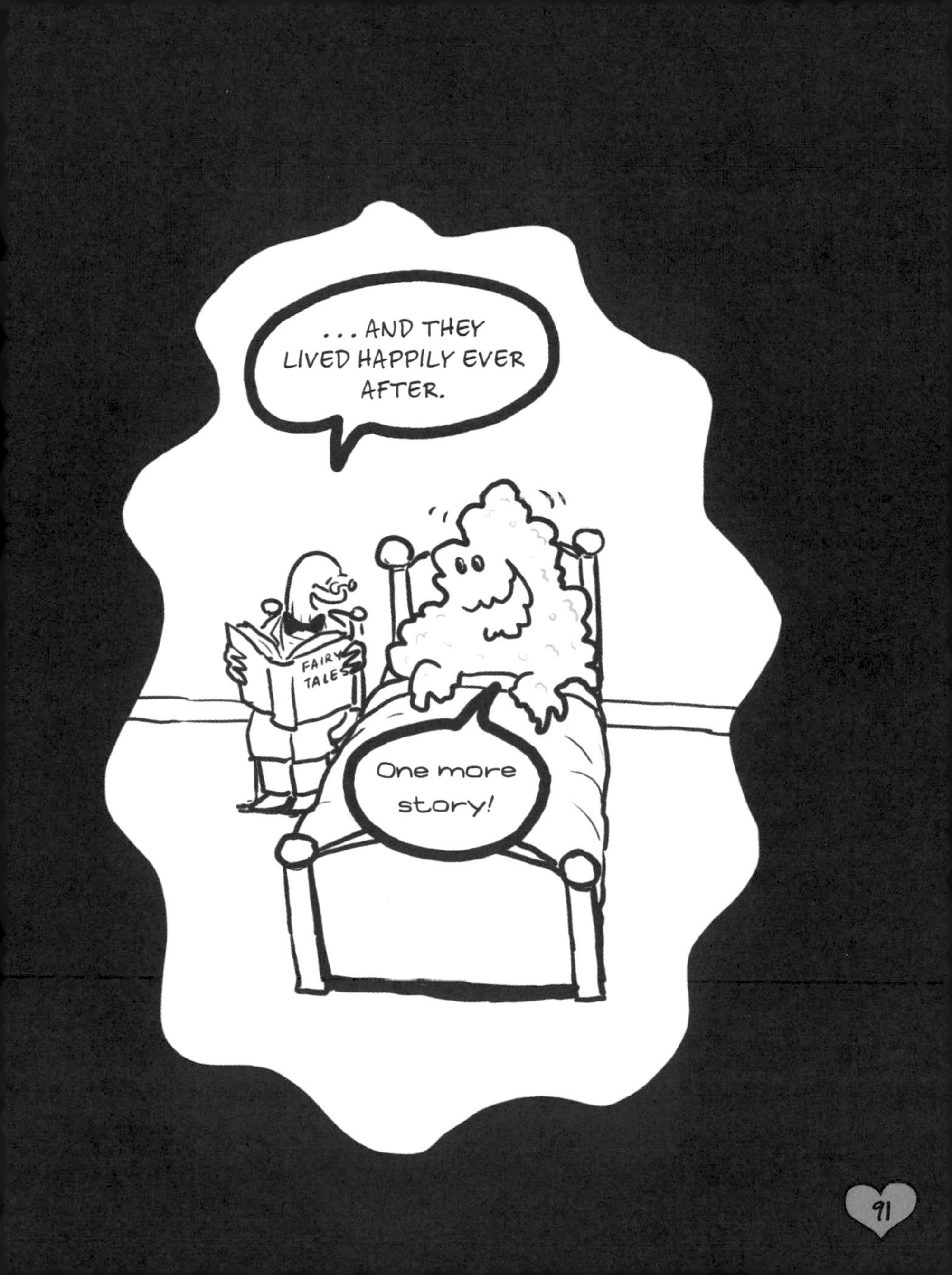

...AND THEY LIVED HAPPILY EVER AFTER.
FAIRY TALES
One more story!

NEW SPECIES!
LEARN ALL THEIR NAMES!

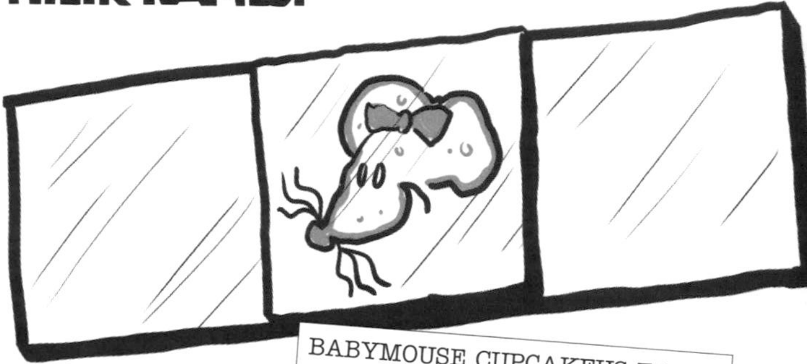

BABYMOUSE CUPCAKEUS EATUS

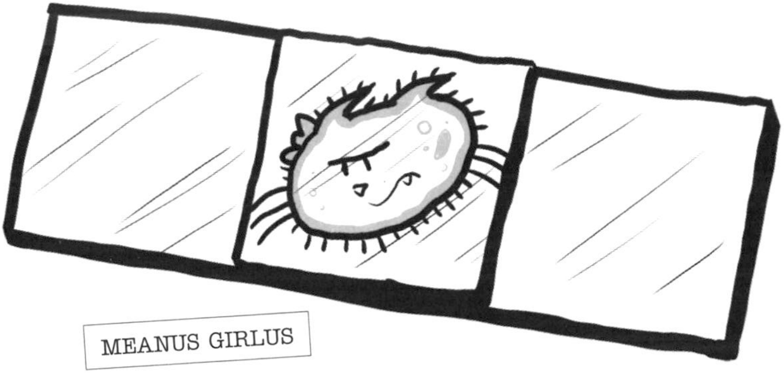

MEANUS GIRLUS

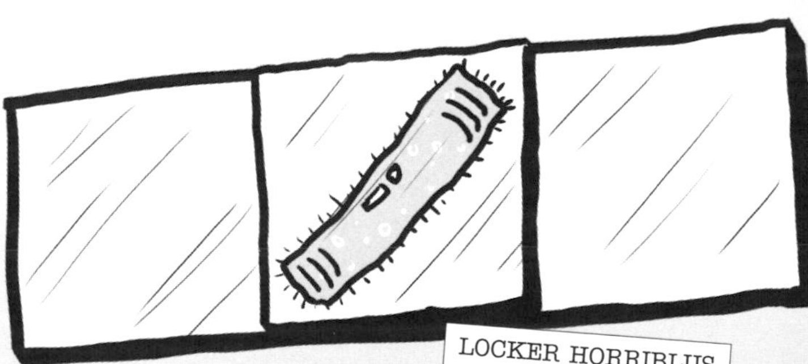

LOCKER HORRIBLUS

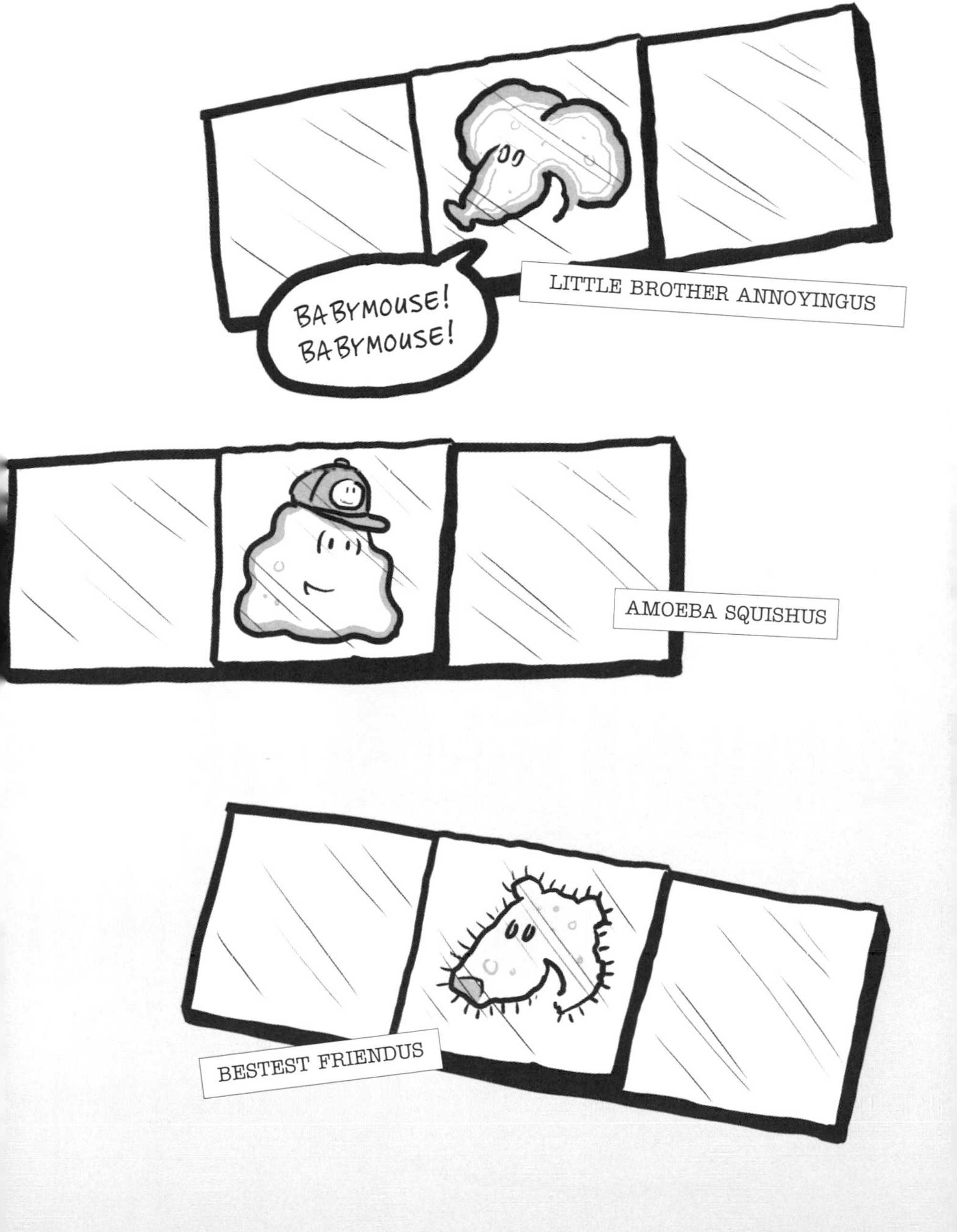
BABYMOUSE! BABYMOUSE!
LITTLE BROTHER ANNOYINGUS
AMOEBA SQUISHUS
BESTEST FRIENDUS

COMING IN FALL 2011!

A VERY BABYMOUSE CHRISTMAS

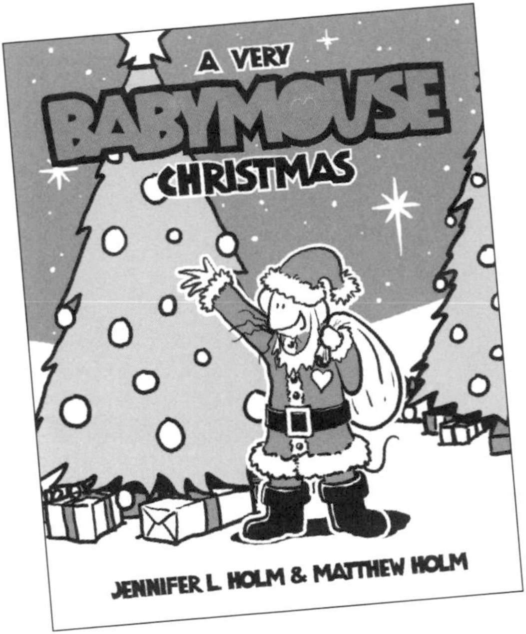
A VERY
BABYMOUSE
CHRISTMAS
JENNIFER L. HOLM & MATTHEW HOLM

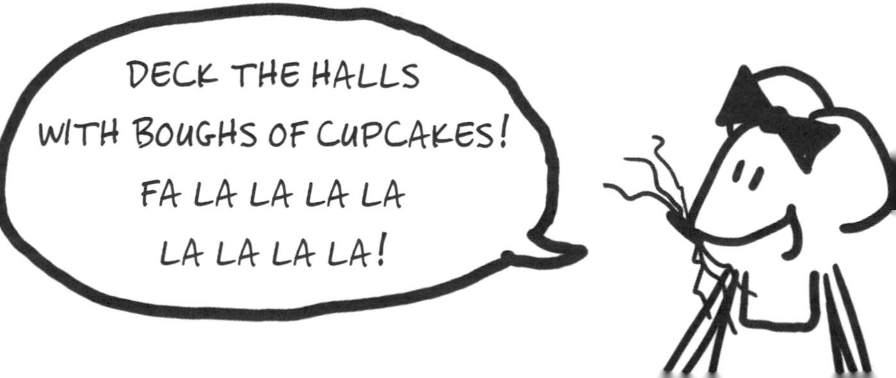
DECK THE HALLS
WITH BOUGHS OF CUPCAKES!
FA LA LA LA LA
LA LA LA LA!

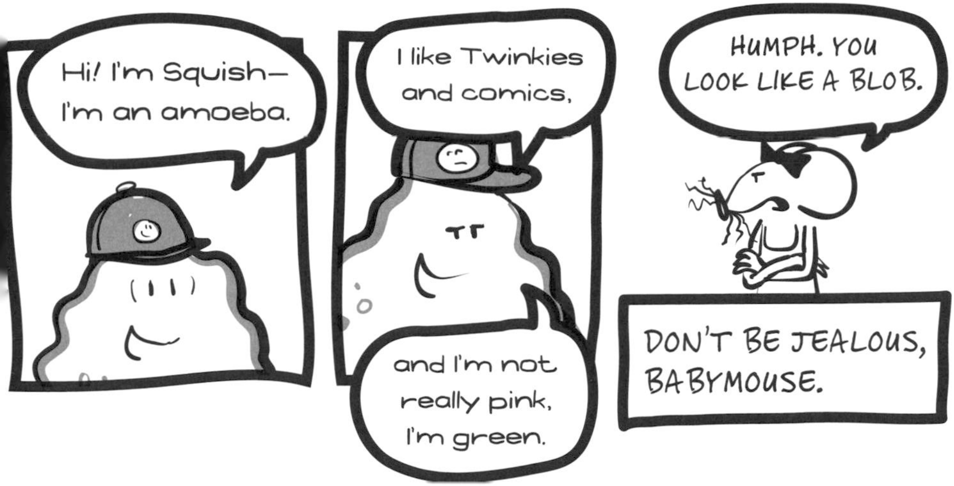
Hi! I'm Squish—
I'm an amoeba.
I like Twinkies
and comics,
and I'm not
really pink,
I'm green.
HUMPH. YOU
LOOK LIKE A BLOB.
DON'T BE JEALOUS,
BABYMOUSE.

READ MORE ABOUT SQUISH'S AMAZING ADVENTURES IN:

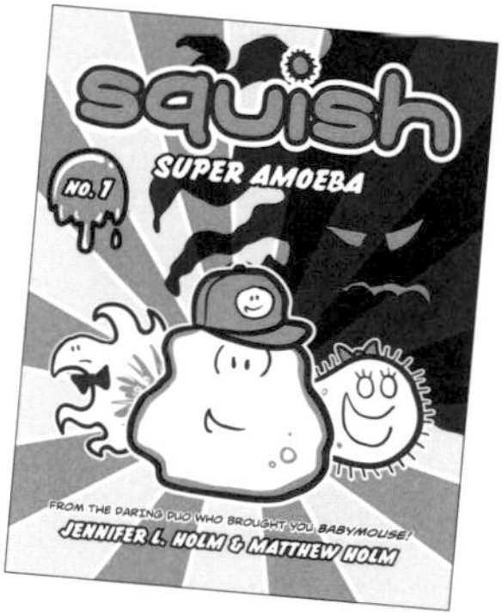
squish
NO. 1
SUPER AMOEBA
FROM THE DARING DUO WHO BROUGHT YOU BABYMOUSE!
JENNIFER L. HOLM & MATTHEW HOLM

AND COMING IN FALL 2011:

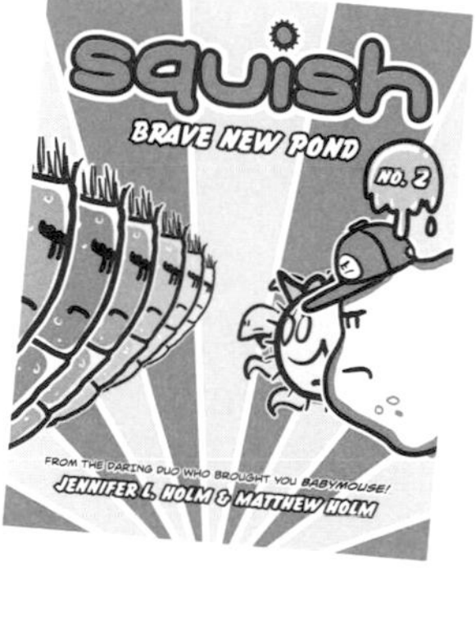
squish
BRAVE NEW POND
NO. 2
FROM THE DARING DUO WHO BROUGHT YOU BABYMOUSE!
JENNIFER L. HOLM & MATTHEW HOLM

If you like Babymouse,
you'll love these other great books
by Jennifer L. Holm!

MIDDLE SCHOOL IS WORSE THAN MEATLOAF
OUR ONLY MAY AMELIA
PENNY FROM HEAVEN
TURTLE IN PARADISE

THEY'RE
REALLY GOOD!
TRUST ME!